SABRINA

AND THE
PURPLE SHOES

By Elsie Limage

ISBN: 978-1-967361-92-2 (sc)
ISBN: 978-1-967361-93-9 (e)

Rev. date: 06/30/2025

CONTENTS

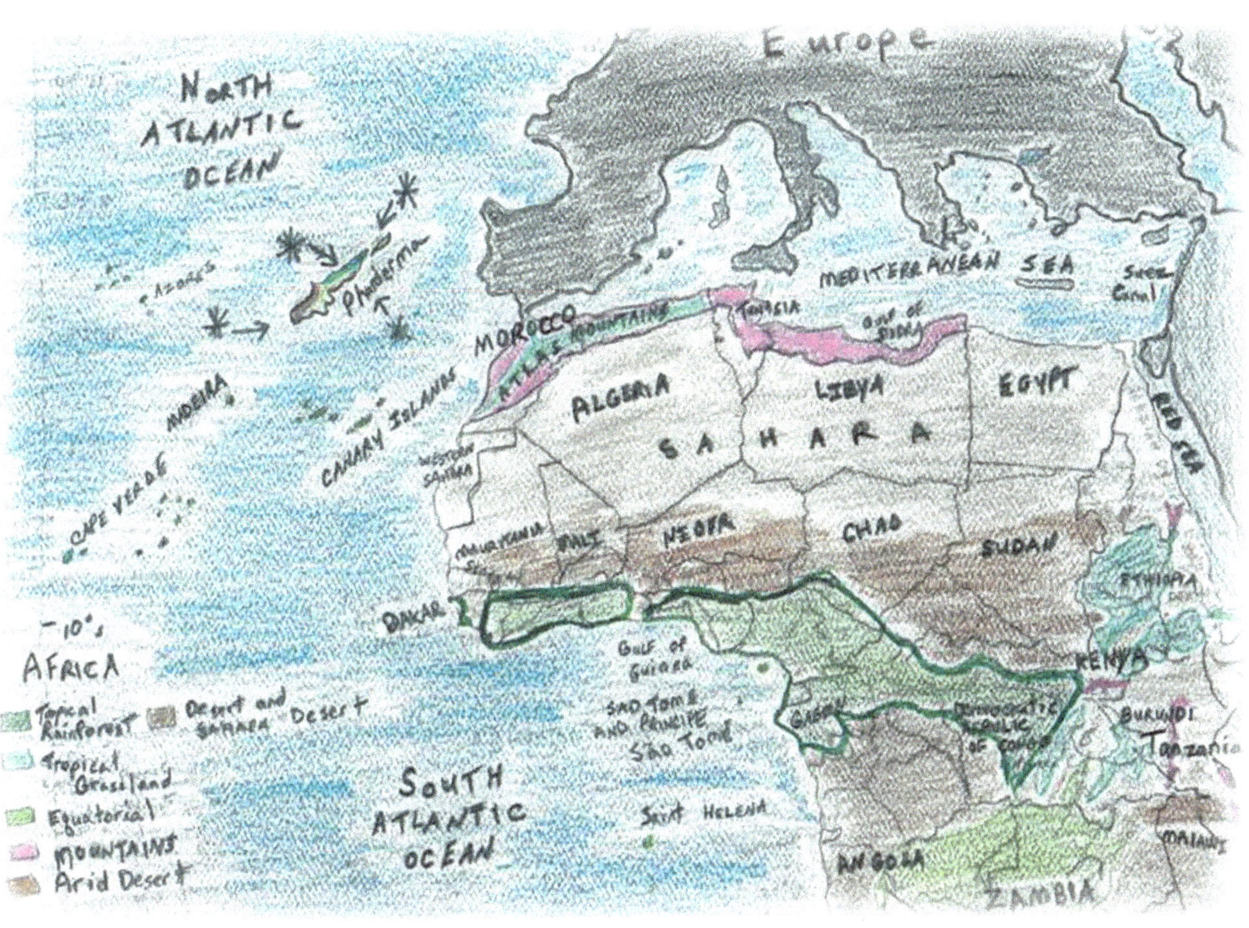

Europe
NORTH ATLANTIC OCEAN
MEDITERRANEAN SEA
Suez Canal
Azores
Phædarnia
MADEIRA
CANARY ISLANDS
CAPE VERDE
MOROCCO
ATLAS MOUNTAINS
TUNISIA
Gulf of Sidra
ALGERIA
LIBYA
EGYPT
SAHARA
WESTERN SAHARA
RED SEA
MAURITANIA
MALI
NIGER
CHAD
SUDAN
ETHIOPIA
DAKAR
Gulf of Guinea
KENYA
SAO TOME AND PRINCIPE
Sao Tomé
GABON
DEMOCRATIC REPUBLIC OF CONGO
BURUNDI
Tanzania
SOUTH ATLANTIC OCEAN
Saint Helena
ANGOLA
ZAMBIA
MALAWI
-10's
AFRICA
Tropical Rainforest
Desert and SAHARA Desert
Tropical Grassland
Equatorial
MOUNTAINS
Arid Desert

CHAPTER ONE

They were out shopping in the Georgia Mall with Grandma Myrtho, Auntie Carmele, and Sabrina's mom, Brigitte. Sabrina was a bright eight-year-old caramel-skinned little girl with the most intelligent and intense eyes, the cutest nose, and oval-shaped face. As they were walking, Sabrina saw a store called Manny's Children's Shoes. Just last week, they were at this very mall, and that store wasn't there. Sabrina was puzzled, then she saw it—the most beautiful purple shoes she had ever seen in her life. Sabrina didn't know what came over her, but she knew she had to have those magnificent sparkling purple shoes.

The magnificent sparkling purple shoes were patent leather with small one-inch heels. On top of the shoe was a beautiful sparkling purple gem, and it seems the shoemaker wanted it to be a butterfly; the wings had blue, purple, and green hues, giving the shoes a magical effect.

Sabrina pulled her mom into the shoe store. Now Brigitte, Sabrina's mom, was a pretty petite woman no more than five feet two inches. Sabrina was a very strong eight-year-old, already almost her mother's height. Brigitte was dreading this so much because she only had twenty dollars on her, and she knew the shoe would be more, and how was she going to disappoint her only daughter? While she was working on something to say, Sabrina had already gotten a salesperson's attention. They were asking her for her shoe size. Sabrina wore a size eight.

The salesperson said, "I'm sorry, but this is our last pair, and it's a size seven."

Well, Sabrina was not going to be deterred; she wanted to try on this shoe so bad she said, "Please may I just try them on? You never know."

Now when the salesperson had said this was the last pair, Brigitte was silently happy, but she managed to put on a sad face.

By the time the salesperson arrived with the shoes, Sabrina's excitement was uncontainable; she felt as if she was coming out of her skin. Up close, she couldn't believe the sheer beauty of the purple shoes, like nothing she had ever seen before. With anticipation, she let the salesperson lift her left foot and her foot slipped in like magic and the shoe fit. Sabrina put her foot down, and she felt like a princess. She looked at the salesperson with glee, and her mom was trying to force a smile. The salesperson asked how it fits.

Sabrina said, "Like a perfect glove."

She tried on the other shoe and felt a complete transformation, like she was a real princess, so now Brigitte asked the salesperson the dreaded question: "How much?"

"Well, you are lucky. This is our last pair, and it is on sale for ten dollars."

Brigitte couldn't believe her ears. She quickly said, "We will take them."

The salesperson took the shoes from Sabrina to ring it up and asked Brigitte if she wanted to participate in their free raffle.

Brigitte said, "Sure."

She filled it out and gave it back, not even taking notice of what the prizes were.

Sabrina wanted to wear the shoes right then and there.

Her mom was telling her that they were going-out shoes and, thus, needed to be saved for only special occasions. "Also Grandma and Auntie Carmele are not done shopping yet. We still have a lot of walking to do," but what Brigitte didn't realize was the shoes fit like sneakers; they were that comfortable.

Sabrina begged, "Please, Mommy, just for today. They fit so well."

In the child's face, Brigitte could sense the urgency of the request and she said, "OK." Well, when they left the store and met back with Grandma and Auntie Carmele, they both started talking at the same time about why Brigitte was letting Sabrina wear those going-out shoes. Brigitte could see that both women were about to start talking a lot, and she said it was her decision and that was it. Both women made faces as if they were about to continue talking. One look at Sabrina's face, the pleading look in her eyes, and both women became quiet.

Well, needless to say, Sabrina's day was wonderful. Every time she looked down at the purple shoes, she felt a total sense of happiness.

That night, tucking her daughter into bed, Brigitte was thinking about her daughter's unnatural reaction to these shoes. Yes, they were beautiful, but Sabrina already had several very pretty shoes. Well, she just shrugged and was happy she could make Sabrina happy. As she looked upon her daughter's face, Sabrina had a smile on her face, and her eyes were moving rapidly under the lids. Brigitte kissed her daughter and said, "Sweet dreams."

CHAPTER TWO

Sabrina was walking through what looked like a palace. She came to a stop because she heard someone crying. Moving toward the sound, she saw a beautiful door, which was so elaborate in its design it looked like the moldings were gold; it shone so bright. There was a big B sign on the front of it. Sabrina pushed the door ajar. What she saw shocked her.

Inside the most beautiful bedroom she has ever seen was a little girl, but what was amazing was the little girl was Sabrina—or looked exactly like Sabrina. The little girl was holding a small crown in her hand, and she was crying soft tears. The little girl had on pretty purple pajamas with golden thread. She was the same caramel color, just like Sabrina, and with a high forehead. Her hair was in finger curls; sometimes Sabrina's mommy would do her hair like that. Sabrina felt a deep sadness for the little girl. *Why was she crying?*

The little girl looked up suddenly and said, "Who's there?"

Sabrina was a little startled now (because she knew she was dreaming). She said, "What? It's my dream." Stepping out of the shadows, she said, "Hello. Why are you crying?"

The girl didn't seem afraid. She looked at Sabrina with wide eyes, and she seemed shocked. Sabrina, sensing her mood, said, "This is a dream...my dream."

The little girl said, "But I'm not dreaming. I'm awake."

Well, Sabrina just shrugged and told herself that this is impossible. Again, she asked the girl, "Why are you crying?"

The girl answered, "My crown! My purple stone is missing from it!" She showed Sabrina her crown, and Sabrina could see where a large hole was; the rest of the crown had smaller stones around it all in different shades of purple.

Instantly, Sabrina remembered her new purple shoes with the large stone in the middle, making the butterfly's body. She wondered, *Could there be a connection?*

The little girl spoke. "Why do you look like me?"

Sabrina said, "I don't know. What's your name?"

The little girl stood on her bed and said, "I am Princess Briana."

Sabrina couldn't believe her ears. *Did she just say Briana?* Sabrina said, "What's your name again?"

The girl repeated. "Briana, and you are?"

Sabrina said, "My name is Sabrina."

Princess Briana said, "Oh, not only do you look like me, but also our names are similar. Why have I not seen you before, and how did you get in here?"

Sabrina told her, "I told you...this is my dream."

Briana said, "You cannot be dreaming because this is really happening to me. I am awake. Well, come closer. I have to see if you are real."

Slowly Sabrina moved toward the magnificent bed. Briana jumped off her bed and stood right in front of her. Sabrina stood very still while Princess Briana walked all round her. Princess Briana said, "We are exactly the same height and everything."

CHAPTER THREE

Suddenly Sabrina could feel something shaking her in her sleep; and in that moment, she woke up. It was her mom waking her up for school; apparently, it was Monday.

"Mommy, I had the most fascinating dream. I was in a castle, and I met a princess named Briana," Sabrina said in excitement.

Sabrina proceeded to tell her mom all about her dream, and Brigitte just listened in awe about her daughter's imagination.

Yet again, Sabrina wanted to wear the purple shoes. Her mom argued that it was a school day. Sabrina pleaded and begged until finally her mom agreed.

At school, everyone complimented Sabrina on her new purple shoes. Sabrina, in all her delight, could not remember ever being happier, nor could she wait for her bedtime. She was anxious to see Princess Briana again (she knew that it was a dream but could not explain how real it felt, and she was sure she can continue this dream). That's why she had really wanted to wear the purple shoes again; she felt the shoes were the connection, and this time she was going to ask Briana more questions. She even wrote a list during her lunch break at school.

Here is the list of questions she is planning on asking Princess Briana:What country are you a princess of?

What are your parents' names?

How old are you?

She was trying to think of more questions to ask her, but all of her friends continuously interrupted her train of thought, asking about her shoes.

When she finally got home, without being told, she did her homework and took a quick shower. She was making sure she did everything so she can go to sleep as fast as possible.

Her grandma noticed all of this commotion going on and noticed she forgot to eat her dinner. She insisted she eat something before going to bed. While she was eating, her mommy came home, looking a little tired. Ever since her parents' divorce, her mother has bad luck on a daily basis. All Sabrina ever wanted was for her mom to be happy. Her daddy, Igor, was happy with his new life. Is it too much to ask for the same for her mom?

She ran and hugged her mom. Brigitte's spirit was immediately lifted from her daughter's greetings. She thanked God every day for giving her this precious little girl.

Sabrina said, "Mommy, everybody...teachers and students...loved my shoes. I don't think I ever want another shoe."

Brigitte said, "But, baby, if you wear the shoes too much, you'll wear it out."

Sabrina said with complete confidence, "No, Mommy, not these shoes—they are special."

Brigitte just shrugged and said, "OK."

Sabrina said, "Mommy, I've had a long day. I'm just so tired. I've done my homework and took my bath, and I've eaten. Can you tuck me in now?"

It was still early; Brigitte didn't get it. *Sabrina asking to go to bed?*

The same kid she had to force every single night is now ready to do so on her own? Brigitte just shook her head and decided to try to make sense of this hurt in her head; she was just going to roll along with it.

So she walked Sabrina to her bedroom and prayed with her and tucked her in.

She asked, "Do you want me to read you a story?"

Sabrina said, "No, Mommy. I'm very sleepy."

Brigitte then kissed her precious child good night.

CHAPTER FOUR

She's in the same huge corridor. She recognized the door to the princess's bedroom (she did it; she was able to continue her dream). Ever so slowly, she pushed the door open. The princess was sitting on her bed, looking like she was waiting for someone.

Their eyes locked, and Briana spoke first with her rich twang. "I knew you would come again. I've been waiting for you."

She got off the bed and walked toward Sabrina. Sabrina proceeded to speak. Briana put up her hand in a halt motion. Sabrina remained quiet.

Briana said, "You must tell me everything about yourself. I found myself thinking only of you today, asking myself, "Was I awake or asleep? Where do you come from? What are your parents' names? What is your age and birthday?"

Sabrina couldn't believe her ears; those where the same questions she was going to ask.

Briana noticed a slight hesitation in Sabrina, and she said, "Come, come. I do not have all night, you know."

Sabrina said, "I come from New York. My mother's name is Brigitte. My father's name is Igor. I am eight years old. My birthday is March 22, 2000."

Briana took a step back, looking at Sabrina differently now with a look of disbelief. She reached out and touched Sabrina's arm. Sabrina, a little taken aback by Briana's reaction, asked her if she was OK.

Briana said, "My parents' names are King Sigor and Queen Gitte. My birthday is March 22, 2000. I am eight years old, and I was born in the land of Pharderma."

Both girls were in shock now, just staring at each other.

Briana spoke first. "I don't understand this. You know, my whole life, I've been asking my mom (the queen) for a sister."

Sabrina said, "Me too."

Briana said, "You say you're dreaming, and I say I'm awake. How is that possible?"

Sabrina decided then to tell her about the purple shoes. "Briana—may I call you Briana?"

Briana said, "You may call me Briana."

"Sunday, my mommy bought me the most magnificent purple shoes I have ever seen. The salesperson told me it was a size seven. I wear a size eight, yet the shoes fit perfectly as if they were magic. When I wear the shoes, I feel magical. I can't begin to describe the feeling—it's wonderful. You see, Briana, on each shoe is a brilliant purple stone. The stone is beautiful, and I believe maybe that it is the same stone missing from your crown. But the confusing part is there are two of the same stones, one for each foot."

Briana said, "I don't understand. I'm only missing one stone from my crown."

Sabrina said, "Where did you get your crown?"

Briana said, "It was my first-year gift from my godmother Lady Elsa. She said she had it made just for me."

CHAPTER FIVE

Again, the shaking; Sabrina's mommy was waking her up again.

"Mommy, guess what—the dream continued from last night." She told her mom the whole dream. Again, Brigitte marveled at her daughter's vivid imagination. Needless to say, she was starting to get concerned about her daughter's behavior and her strange fascination to the shoes. She didn't want her daughter thinking that life was a fairy tale.

Sabrina could sense her mom's disbelief. Then it hit her that Princess Briana's godmother was named Elsa, and her godmother's name was Elsie—again too close for comfort. She made a mental note to ask Briana if her godmother was her mom's sister just like hers.

Again, Sabrina insisted on wearing the purple shoes. Brigitte just gave up trying to convince her daughter that those shoes were for going out only. She even pointed out to Sabrina that she didn't have that much to match the shoes, but it seems nothing worked; matching or not matching, Sabrina had to wear her purple shoes.

That day in school, Sabrina told one of her teachers about her dreams. She could see the disbelief in her teacher's eyes. *Why does no one believe this?* It made her a little sad, but it was only for a moment; the shoes just kept her happy. She kept wondering, *What does a princess do all day long? Did she go to school?* Questions, questions, and more questions, but no answers. Sabrina was getting frustrated. Again, she marveled that she wasn't even sleepy because her dream seemed so real; Briana even touched her, and she was real.

Finally, school was over. Grandma Myrtho picked her up. It was Tuesday, and that meant McDonald's. Sabrina usually was excited, but this time, all she wanted to do was to go back to bed. Grandma seemed in no hurry to return home; she even wanted Sabrina to go to church with her. That meant she wouldn't be in bed until 9:00 p.m. Oh! The anticipation she was feeling was just too much, so she decided to tell Grandma about her dreams. After Sabrina finished her recollection of the dreams, Grandma just said, "You are just like your auntie Elsie, always making up stories." Then it clicked. She wanted to kiss her grandma. Who else but Auntie Elsie would believe her? Didn't Auntie Elsie give birth to her cousin Jean Paul at home and somehow was prewarned?

Sabrina just knew her auntie Elsie was the key, and maybe Briana's godmother Elsa was the other key. She was getting more and more excited by the second, and to think she wouldn't be in bed until 9:00 p.m. Usually, when Sabrina went to church with her grandma, she would fall asleep; but this time she was too excited; she was wide awake and alert.

The pastor speaking this evening was Brother Carlo, a good friend of Grandma. He was talking about faith—that faith was the key to it all. Finally, she was being tucked into bed by her mommy with a kiss on the cheek. Sabrina was out like a light.

CHAPTER SIX

This time, she found Briana outside the door, sitting down. Briana looked like she just saw a ghost. Sabrina walked up to her slowly, waving her hand in front of Briana's face. Finally, Briana snapped out of whatever trance she was in. Briana looked at her and said, "I wanted to know where you came from. I have been sitting here, waiting for you to see what direction you came from, and it seems you just appeared out of thin air."

Sabrina could not answer that question; she didn't know, so she just shrugged. That didn't make Briana happy.

Sabrina said, "I have more questions for you."

Briana said, "Me too."

As soon as they got inside, Sabrina asked her, "Your godmother— what is she for your mom?"

Briana said, "She's my mom's sister. Why do you ask?"

"Because, Briana, I have an auntie Elsie, who also happens to be my mom's sister."

"You know, Sabrina, my godmother is the one that gave me the purple-stoned crown. Maybe she can help us unlock whatever is going on here. I don't think I should tell my mom and dad since they are the king and queen. You are actually trespassing. I will ask my mom to take me to see my godmother tomorrow."

Sabrina said, "I won't be able to see my godmother because she lives in New York, yet I can always call her on Saturday."

Briana said, "That's OK," and took Sabrina's hand.

They interlocked their fingers, and Sabrina felt something she couldn't understand;

she felt complete, more complete than when she wore the purple shoes, more than playing with her cousins or mommy—a new feeling—and it seemed Briana felt it too because she looked at Sabrina in the strangest way.

There was relief in her soul, in something bigger than what man has made. In Sabrina's soul, she knew there was more to these dreams, these shoes. She had to keep her faith and believe in her instinct, and her instinct was telling her all of this was not a big coincidence.

CHAPTER SEVEN

Again, the shaking; her mommy waking her up—again! Sabrina decided she didn't want to tell her mom about the dream this time; she felt quiet and complete. This was too much. She needed help, and the finger was pointing toward her auntie Elsie. She asked her mom at breakfast if they could visit Auntie Elsie this weekend. Her mom said, "Sure, baby," happy that Sabrina wasn't rattling about another dream because she was starting to worry about her daughter.

CHAPTER EIGHT

Meanwhile, in a faraway land, Princess Briana asked her mom, Queen Gitte, if she could see her godmother Elsa. Queen Gitte was delighted that her daughter asked about anything because ever since Monday, her daughter had been acting withdrawn. She granted her wish immediately.

Her sister (Briana's godmother) lived in a beautiful house on the outside of town. She had three kids of her own—Vlad, Rena, and JP, short for Jean-Pierre. Her sister's husband's name was Paulo; he was a rich merchant, having made his fortune early on with rare gems from Africa, Siberia, Madagascar, and the deep Atlantic Ocean. Briana's auntie Elsa always fascinated her. In a land where women were always criticized, auntie stayed true to herself, always wearing whatever she wanted, and she had a passion for all types of jewelry. Auntie Elsa and her mom looked so different from each other. Briana's mom was a pretty petite, busty, light-skinned woman, and Auntie Elsa was also pretty and of regular height and a darker caramel complexion than Briana. Briana also had two other aunts, Auntie Sigrid and Auntie Bebin. She didn't see them that much, and they both lived very far away.

Sometimes Briana wished they lived closer because they both had daughters. Briana was so lonely. Her cousin Rena was nine years older than her; plus, she was so tall—taller than her auntie Elsa. Sometimes Briana's neck would hurt looking up at her.

The car stopped; they have arrived. Briana always felt happy when she went to her aunt's house. Their house was alive with laughter and cheer. Sometimes the castle was so very cold. Before Briana knew, the door flew open. It was Rena.

She yelled, "Munchkin!"

Every time Briana came over, her cousin had a different nickname for her. She was picked up and swung around.

Rena was crazy about her little princess cousin. Briana was the essence of adorable, with her deep, smooth caramel skin, her almond-shaped eyes, and her small frame. Briana was a beautiful child. Finally, Briana was set back on her feet.

She said, "Where is Auntie Elsa?"

Rena just yelled, "Mommy! Briana is here."

Auntie Elsa came rushing downstairs to greet her. Again, she was picked and kissed all over her face. "So how is my little Boh Boh?" Her godmother also had strange names for her.

"I'm fine, Auntie. I just wanted to see you."

"OK. Let's go to the kitchen. I made all your favorites. Your mom called and said you asked to spend the day with us."

In the kitchen, there were noodles and sausage, chocolate cake with fudge icing, and Oreo cookies.

Briana just realized she was hungry, and she sat and enjoyed a little of everything. Auntie was just sitting across from her, watching her eat. Rena had disappeared into her teenage world, and it was either the phone or the Internet. Well, Briana didn't mind; she did want to speak to her auntie in private.

After she took the last bite of her favorite cake, she said, "Auntie Elsa, something strange has been happening these past few days." She told her auntie everything that happened since Sunday night.

Auntie Elsa never disturbed her; she just listened with wide eyes. After she finished recollecting everything that had happened, her auntie said, "Have you seen the purple shoes?"

Briana couldn't believe her ears; her auntie didn't think she was crazy—she believed her. "No, Auntie, I haven't seen the shoes. She is always barefoot and in her pajamas."

Auntie Elsa told Briana, "If she comes tonight, tell her she must come the next night with the shoes on."

"OK, Auntie."

Then Auntie said something that shocked Briana:

"I'm sleeping over tonight in your room. I want to see this for myself."

Wow, her aunt, in the eight years she's been alive, never slept in the castle; even when there were balls, she always went home. So with that settled, Briana spent the rest of the afternoon playing games with Rena. They colored and played word games. Briana loved being in her aunt's house.

CHAPTER NINE

Meanwhile, her aunt Elsa had closed herself up in her bedroom; she was recollecting the past.

Her sister, Queen Gitte, was in labor. She was having horrible pains. Her screams vibrated the whole castle. King Sigor was screaming at everyone. One last scream, the baby came out, and the queen passed out from exhaustion. The doctor took the baby—nothing—no movement, no breath. The queen had given birth to a stillborn child. The king had gone crazy. He took the doctor aside. They spoke behind closed doors. The king came out and grabbed Elsa into his study. He told Elsa that she had to bury the dead child and she had to swear on the Bible that she never saw this, that it never happened, or he said her precious children, Vlad, Rena, and Jean-Pierre, would be in danger, so Elsa was forced to swear to this awful secret.

This secret made her heart heavy every day. By the time her sister Gitte woke up, she immediately asked to see her baby; and miraculously, a baby was brought to her. Elsa looked at the baby and wondered, *Where did they get this baby from?* Every day, she listened to the news. *Maybe someone is looking for their child or maybe a mother died at childbirth or maybe they had taken a twin?*

Questions, questions, but never an answer. Only the king and the doctor knew the truth. Elsa never dared to ask either.

A long time ago, Elsa had felt that the only reason no one had ever had a missing baby report was either (1) an unwed mother had died at her childbirth or (2) they had taken a twin.

When her husband had come home from an expedition in Siberia with the most beautiful deep-purple amethyst stones, there were two stones that where identical to each other.

Elsa started working on her plan. With one stone, she had made Briana the most beautiful crown and had given it to her on her first birthday; the crown was made to adjust as the child aged. The other stone she had saved in her safe, waiting for something—anything—to happen. Well, six months ago, on a trip with her husband in America, they stayed in New York City at the Limage Hotel, one of New York's most beautiful hotels. She and her husband went to a popular restaurant called the Olive Garden. There was a big party going on. Then she saw her—Briana's duplicate.

It seemed to be a baby shower. A very pregnant lady with long hair was at the foot of the table, and there was Briana's duplicate. Elsa looked for Briana's mom, and—oh my god! It was uncanny that Briana's mom looked just like her sister, and there was a dark woman with long hair that looked like her. She felt a chill go down her spine.

She knew in her heart that this child had to be Briana's twin; she had to come up with a plan.

She had to find out at least one person's name in that table. All the time her husband's talking to her, she's paying close attention to the party table. They signaled for the waitress to bring the check. She saw that the woman that looked like her pulled out a credit card and gave it to the waitress. Immediately, she told her husband she had to go to the bathroom. Instead, she followed the waitress and told the waitress that she wished to pay their bill. The waitress was a little shocked, yet people in New York did do these things; so she opened the billfold, and Elsa noticed the name on the credit card and was a little shocked that the person's name was Elsie Limage ([1] her name was Elsa and [2] they were staying at the L'image Hotel—coincidence). Somehow Elsa was believing that they are no coincidences ever.

She hurried back to her table. By now, her husband had noticed that his wife wasn't paying much attention to him for some reason; she was paying more attention to her surrounding environment. *Well,* he told himself. *It is her first time in New York—she's fascinated.*

Elsa watched closely as the waitress went back to the table to tell Elsie that her bill was paid in full. In horror, she noticed the waitress was about to point to her. She grabbed the menu to hide her face and told her husband they have to go now. She put on her shades. Paulo was confused; he hadn't gotten his dessert or coffee. She was really acting strange.

He said, "Why are you in such a hurry?"

She told him, "I have a surprise for you back at the hotel." Elsa knew exactly what to say to him because he loved surprises. No longer confused, he got up right away.

The next day, she found a private investigator in the yellow pages named Shane Braham. His advertisement mentioned he could find anyone and anything. She asked him to check which children were born on March 22, 2000, at 2:00 p.m. to Black or multiracial parents. She paid him handsomely to be very discreet.

She was to be in New York for only one more week. She told her husband she wanted to stay another week, to go home without her. He hesitated; he didn't like the idea of leaving his beautiful wife alone in a big city. She told him several of her college friends lived in New York and she wanted to catch up with them.

He had to go back to Pharderma; he had a big business meeting that he could not miss.

It took the investigator exactly one week to find every child born to ethnic parents that day; 139 children were born at the same time. It took him three days to find Brigitte St. Phard and Sabrina St. Phard. Brigitte was a divorcee living with her daughter and mother in Queens, and her ex-husband lived in Pennsylvania. She had to think of a plan fast—what to do, how was she going to connect these two kids because many times. She had looked deep in Briana's eyes and seen a deep, deep sadness; no child should know so much sorrow and, worse, not know why the sorrow even existed.

She knew whatever she came up with could be dangerous, but if it could happen by accident, no one would ever know the part she played in it. Elsa was so tired of thinking. She went to bed exhausted. While sleeping, she had a dream of purple shoes with the brilliant amethyst stones she had; each shoe had a stone. She woke up that morning refreshed, with a plan. She would make the most beautiful shoes any little girl would fall in love with.

There were holes in her plan—how on God's green earth would the right little girl pick the shoe? In her heart and in her soul, she knew only one little girl could have these shoes. Elsa felt a strange sense of confidence that she wasn't alone; someone—something bigger—was helping her, so she proceeded with her plan. Well, first, she had to get Briana's stone from her crown. How was she going to do that?

The opportunity came a week later. King Sigor announced he was going to have a ball for his brother, Prince Stranoff, who was visiting for a short while. That night, she would steal the stone from the princess's crown, which she had given her on her first birthday. No one would suspect her. She had to move fast. The investigator informed her that Brigitte St. Phard and her daughter, Sabrina, were planning a trip to Georgia. She had a brother named Charlie. They were going to visit for one week. A chill went down her spine. The family—they were like her own family; the similarities were uncanny, to say the least, because she too had a brother—in fact two brothers, one named Karlie and the other was Keycil, and Brigitte's brothers' names were Charlie and Cecil.

The similarities were starting to freak her out. That night at the ball, Briana looked so beautiful. She was wearing a lavender dress. She was every inch the princess she was with the beautiful crown that her godmother had given her; meanwhile, Briana did have other crowns that the king had given her, but she never wore the other crowns. She always wears the one her godmother gave her.

After midnight, the other small children were taken home, and Briana was taken to her room by her mommy and tucked into bed. The crown was left on the nightstand by Briana's bed. After the queen left her daughter's room, Elsa crept in. The child was asleep. With the precision of a jeweler, she pried the stone from its setting.

She let the crown fall behind the nightstand. Tucking the stone into her bosom, she went to her husband and said she was exhausted and if they can go home. Her husband never really liked the king too much; he was more than happy to take his lovely wife home. There was something about the king he didn't like but couldn't put his finger on it. The very next day, Elsa went to her shoemaker. She wanted him to make the most beautiful children's shoes ever made; it had to be purple, and it had to have purple stones on it.

She asked him if he had any purple stones. He said yes and showed her two glass purple stones. She was delighted and asked when the shoes will be ready. He said he had several other orders before her—about two weeks.

Elsa pulled out a large wad of cash and said, "I want it in two days, and they have to be perfect."

He looked at the cash with wide eyes. Reaching out his arm to take it, Elsa moved it back out of his reach and said, "You must give me your word. You will have half now and the other half upon completion."

"Miss, you have my word," He agreed greedily.

Elsa walked away with a smile. There were still flaws in the plan, but something told her everything will be OK. For some reason, it seemed as if two days were like two months with the anticipation in Elsa's stomach. Finally, they were ready!

She walked into the shoemaker's shop, and he had a wide smile on his face. He pulled out a purple box, and inside—Elsa took a deep breath in—the shoemaker had outdone himself, and the shoes were exactly what she saw in her dream: deep purple platinum leather, low heels with a beautiful butterfly on the foot of each shoe; the wings were purple, green, and black, and the body was the glass purple stones. Elsa gave the shoemaker the rest of the money. As soon as she got home, she ran to her bedroom and locked the door. She opened her safe. Inside, the real stones shone so bright she was momentarily blinded.

Carefully she took the stones out and marveled at the magnificence of God's work. Elsa couldn't remember seeing two stones so brilliant, so flawless in her life; in fact, they were unusually brilliant. Elsa took her special jewelry glasses and took a good look at the stones. To Elsa's astonishment, it seemed inside the stones had what looked like a small flame, as if the stones themselves were alive!

She held each stone in her hands. Suddenly she was moving through space. She found herself where Sabrina and her mom where staying in Suwanee, Georgia, and Brigitte was telling her daughter that on Sunday, they would be going to the mall with Auntie Carmele and Grandma because Grandma wanted to buy a few things before their flight back to New York because Monday was school. It seems Elsa could see them, but they were not aware that someone else was in the room. She stood there a little longer and watched Sabrina converse with her mom. She thought she was prying on their privacy, and next thing she knew, she was back in her bedroom.

Back in her bedroom, she put the stones down, looking at them and wondering where exactly her husband got these stones. Mental note: As soon as he comes home, she will ask him. She went to work, switching the glass stones for the real ones. Upon completion, as beautiful the shoes were with the glass stones, with the real stones, now they took on a new dimension of beauty all their own; it was as if the shoes had come alive!

She heard the downstairs door open and looked at the time; it was 5:00 p.m. Her husband was home. She hoped he had a good memory. She ran downstairs as he walked in. She was always glad to see her husband even after twenty-three years of marriage. He was such a handsome man. He had dark-brown skin, almond-shaped eyes, with eyelashes longer than her own. His nose was broad, and he had the sweetest lips. Yes, she was always glad to see him.

"Darling, how are you?"

Paulo looked up, and his beautiful wife was approaching him with a big smile.

He was always happy to see her happy, and today she radiated with happiness. A big hug and kiss.

"Sweetie, I want to jog your memory a little bit. Remember, eight years ago, you gave me two identical deep-purple amethyst stones and many smaller stones in a small pouch? Can you tell me where you got them?"

Paulo remembered exactly how he came by owning the stones; he would never forget.

"I was fishing in Lake Victoria, Africa, and a small child was playing by the water. I could see he was not alone. An old woman was watching him. It happened so fast. One minute, the child was playing. The next, he was in the water, drowning. I acted on impulse and jumped in and pulled the boy out. He had already swallowed a good amount of water. The old woman was standing at the edge. I put the boy down and gave him mouth-to-mouth recitation, and he came back, coughing up water. The old woman was crying. She was speaking a strange dialect. She bent down and hugged the child. I was overwhelmed and just happy the boy was OK. I touched her shoulder to comfort her.

"She took my hand in hers and said, 'Or, or.' I couldn't understand her words. She had a pouch around her waist, and she showed me what was in it—the two large amethyst stones and several small stones also, all amethyst. Putting them all back into the pouch, she put the pouch in my hands. She covered her hands on mine and kept repeating these words, *'Adonai ori v'yishi mimi irah.'* This means 'God is my light and my salvation; whom shall I fear?' Then she took my face in her hands and kissed me on each cheek, forehead, and chin. When she let go of me, I looked in her eyes, and I didn't see an old lady. I saw pure joy and happiness and something else. I can't, until this day, say what I felt and saw in her eyes. All I know is I felt at bliss with the entire world. My soul was happy."

Elsa was shocked. He had never told her that story before. *What was the something else that he saw in the old woman's eyes?* Questions, questions, so many questions. Well, she knew the stones had power. She was about to tell her husband about the stones' power yet decided against it. He had a businessman mind; his first thought would be to sell it to the highest bidder. No, this would be her secret.

It was Wednesday, and she had to move fast, or she might miss her chance. She thought of sending the shoes by mail to the private investigator. She couldn't risk losing them; it had to be her. What would she tell her husband? He would want to know why she needed to go to America again so soon since their return six months ago. The answer came in a phone call from an old classmate, and guess what?

She lived in Georgia, in Gwinnett County. She was being honored for a book she had written, and it was being held in Atlanta, Georgia, at the historical Ebenezer Baptist Church (where Dr. Martin Luther King became an ordained minister). Elsa's husband was home when the phone call came. He was listening in on the conversation. Already he felt himself getting angry; he was busy the whole weekend with meetings, and here somebody was inviting his beautiful wife halfway around the world. He was not happy at all.

As expected, while on the phone, she held the receiver in one hand and spoke to him.

"Darling, do you remember my roommate in college, Jartine? Well, she lives in America and has invited me to this important event. Darling, please let's go."

He shook his head no, and Elsa put her best pleading face on. She had to go to America!

"Darling, I will be back on Monday. It's only for four days."

Oh, he hated that face. Well, what really could he do but let her go? "OK, baby, enjoy yourself."

She told Jartine she would be delighted to attend. Jartine insisted on her staying at her home. At first, it sounded like a good idea, but Elsa said, "No, thank you." She had too many things to do, let alone have to answer to her friend if she needed to go out and do errands. She immediately called the airport to book a flight for the next day.

Things were moving fast. The first thing she packed was the purple shoes. She had to open the box to just look at them again. She had called the private investigator, and he was to meet her in a café at the airport with Sabrina's photos. They were not to speak to each other directly, just in case someone recognized her. She had the king to worry about and her husband. The last thing she needed was to be seen speaking to a strange man.

That night, Elsa couldn't sleep. Her mind was plagued with questions, and her nerves were shot. Her plan was to get the photos and rent a car. Elsa booked her hotel in Atlanta. Jartine lived in Dallas, Georgia. Sabrina was visiting Suwanee, Georgia. If anyone questions her, she wanted to visit the capital of Georgia.

She was taking the Concord; flight time was 8:00 a.m. and arrival at 12:00 p.m. in Atlanta, Georgia. Finally, daylight seeped into her room; it was 5:00 a.m., and Elsa didn't get a wink of sleep. She rechecked her luggage and everything was set—the wig, glasses, even padded bra and underpants, and, last, the precious purple shoes. The shoes were placed in her carry-on luggage; she was keeping it close, leaving nothing to chance.

When Elsa went down to breakfast, the maid had her favorite fresh bread, eggs over easy, ham, and banana—her all-time favorite breakfast. She discovered she was unusually hungry and ate all the food, not sure what the plane would be serving. Yep, she wasn't taking any chances. Her husband came down, fully dressed and annoyed that he would be driving her to the airport himself. Wow, he always used a chauffeur; Elsa even forgot he was actually able to drive. Knowing her husband and his jealous streak, he always thought that she was up to something. Well, yes, Elsa was always up to something, yet it was never what he thought. Anyway, what a nice feeling. After twenty-three years with the same woman, a man can still feel uneasy. A smile came across her face.

"What are you smiling about?" Paulo asked.

"Well, it's just nice to know you still are crazy about me." He kissed her forehead, still not thrilled about her going; plus, for some reason, he felt she was up to something, having already checked out the place Jartine was getting honored at, and it was real. Something just wasn't right, and he couldn't put his finger on it.

"Darling, what time is your flight?"

"At 8:00 a.m."

It was six twenty. He would have to eat breakfast quickly; the airports were crazy these days.

Paulo got out one of his favorite cars, the Bentley Continental R, an absolutely beautiful car. It was a lovely November morning. The drive to the airport was quiet, and there was no traffic.

At last, Elsa was on the plane, finally situated with her bag with the shoes on her lap, too paranoid to leave it in the upper bin. Feeling the exhaustion seeping through her body, she fell into a deep sleep. When she opened her eyes, the pilot was announcing to "please put your seat belts back on." Looking down, her seat belt was securely fastened; she had never taken it off.

Getting off the plane, she collected her luggage and went to find the café the investigator said he would be. She found it right away. Seeing the investigator sitting exactly where he said he would be, she grabbed a menu, waiting for him to notice her. Right away, he got up and left the café. They never even looked at each other. Immediately Elsa went and sat in his newly vacant spot, sitting right on the manila folder that the investigator had conveniently left for her. With a fast-beating heart, the excitement was so intense, now she knew what being a spy felt like; they must lead very exciting lives. Suddenly she was famished. She ordered some food, and while eating, she casually dropped her napkin; and while picking it up, she grabbed the manila folder. In one slick move, she placed it in her open bag by her foot. It was all done so smoothly. Yes, she did have a knack for this type of stuff. This was fun!

Finished with her meal, she paid the waitress and left a regular tip. She didn't want anyone to remember her; leaving too large of a tip would cause the waitress to remember her. Now to get her rental car. She hoped it also had a GPS because she had never been in Georgia before. At the rental center, it cost her an extra $200 for a car with the GPS system; money wasn't an object. She wanted to get a luxury car yet decided against. She had to keep a low profile—best to stay unnoticed. If anyone noticed her and if King Sigor were to find out what she was up to, it would definitely mean an execution. Even though the threat was there, she was compelled to do this; something bigger than Elsa was guiding her as if she was a puppet. It took Elsa forty-five minutes to arrive at her hotel. She had reserved a regular room, and she was only spending four days.

Not bothering to unpack, sitting on the bed, she took the yellow manila folder and took out the pictures of Sabrina, her mom Brigitte, Uncle Charlie and his wife, Carmele, and Grandma Myrtho, also Charlie's three boys, Joshua, Luke, and Emmanuel. Looking at the photographs of the family, she couldn't help noticing the similarities to her own family; it was freaky. Elsa's own mother's name was Yrtho, her brothers Karlie and Keycil. Keycil, her much younger brother, was the renegade of the family; he just had too much going on in his life.

Looking at Sabrina's picture, she pulled out pictures she carried of Briana. *Wow, identical twins! They must find each other.* Elsa had purchased a map of Suwanee, Georgia; they had three malls close to them and one huge mall thirty minutes away. She had to know which mall they would be going to. Elsa had to use the stones again. Pulling the shoes out, she concentrated hard on what she wanted.

Again she was moving through space. She was in Charlie and Carmele's house; everyone was sitting in the living room, talking.

Myrtho asked Carmele, "Which mall will you be taking us to on Saturday, the big one or the small one?"

"Mommy, I'm taking you to the small one because the big one is just too far."

Myrtho said, "OK, that's not a problem. I just want to get a few things."

Brigitte replied, "I'm not even trying to get anything. I only have twenty dollars to my name."

Carmele asked Brigitte, "When you get back to New York, are you going to look for another job?"

Brigitte replied, "Of course. I'm not getting paid enough with my current job."

Elsa concentrated on going back to her hotel room, and she was back. The power of the stones were unbelievable. Pulling out her laptop, she put in the Suwanee address and found the closest mall to their home. Tomorrow she would drive to the mall and check it out.

The cell phone rang; it was her husband, and he asked why she didn't pick up the phone earlier. Elsa guessed when you're traveling with the stones, cell phones don't work because it was in her pants pocket. What could she tell him?

He definitely wouldn't believe what she was really doing, so she told him that she had been in the shower.

He answered, "OK. I just wanted to make sure you got there safely. What are you going to do today?"

"I thought I would call Jartine and find out if she was free and hook up with her. How are the kids doing?"

"They're OK. Rena wanted to know why you didn't take her. She said she's never been to America and this is your second time."

"I guess Rena forgot she has school."

Paulo just laughed. "OK, I'll pass that along."

"Bye, love."

"Sweetie, always be safe. Make sure you are aware of your surroundings. Don't walk with your head down."

Elsa laughed. "OK, love, I'll be aware of everything. Bye-bye."

Elsa closed the phone and just shook her head. *He doesn't even know I'm watching everything. My senses have heightened since I started this adventure.*

She called Jartine. The answering machine came on, leaving a message that she was in town.

Well, if she has nothing to do, might as well check out the mall. Thank God the car has GPS. What a wonderful invention.

Driving through Georgia, Elsa marveled at the size of just one state in America. Pharderma was such a small island of the North Atlantic Ocean. Everyone knew everyone. Elsa loved the closeness of the island; a person can get lost in such a huge country.

She arrived at the mall.

Wow, they call this a small mall?

There was a huge Target, Marshalls, KB Toys, Manny's Children's Shoes, several restaurants, hair salons, and two bookstores.

She headed straight for Manny's Children's Shoes, a nice-size shoe store with a great selection of shoes, and a salesperson came over.

"May I help you, madam?"

There was something about being called madam that didn't rub too well with Elsa; it made her feel old. She decided to ignore the word and told the salesperson she was just browsing, studying the place, taking mental notes of all the seats and mirrors. Elsa wondered if she should speak to the manager of this place but decided against that idea.

Better to take it by surprise. Giving them too much information too soon would give them time to think about what will happen.

With her plan set in her mind, she headed out back to the car. Just then, Jartine called and invited her to her house for dinner.

Elsa drove back to her hotel to relax before driving to Dallas, Georgia, for dinner. Back at the hotel, Elsa was thinking about writing her whole plan down, then she thought against that, leaving it in her mind. She was safer from prying eyes.

At Jartine's home, Elsa met her daughter for the first time. Ophelia was very tall and a stunner. Jartine lived alone with her daughter in a huge house. It was almost as big as Elsa's mansion, but Elsa lived with her husband and three kids, a maid, and a chauffeur. This house was so quiet; even outside was quiet you could hear a pin drop.

Jartine was telling Elsa she didn't understand why she wasn't staying at her house, why she had to stay at a hotel when she had told her about the amount of space she had. Elsa couldn't possibly tell her the real reason. She just said Atlanta was closer to some touring she wanted to do, plus Atlanta was much closer to the airport. Jartine seemed to accept that and didn't bring the subject up again. They talked for hours, catching up on life since the university. Elsa was happy Jartine was doing so well on her own. It was getting late, and Elsa announced she had to leave. Jartine told her she should sleep the night, but Elsa insisted on leaving.

Back at her hotel, she was curious to see what was happening in the Baptiste household. She took the shoes out, and *wham*—she was there. This time, Sabrina was being tucked in bed by her mom. Elsa just watched as Brigitte took a book out—it was *Cinderella*—and read to Sabrina. Elsa remembered telling her own daughter that story, yet she thought it was quite fitting. Suddenly she felt as if she was disturbing them, so she wished herself back.

Back at the hotel, she had to continue with her plan. The next day, she had to make some purchases. She needed a small printer and some raffle tickets. Checking her laptop, she located an OfficeMax about ten minutes away from the hotel; they would have everything she needed.

She woke from a wonderful dream but couldn't remember one thing, yet she felt at peace. Taking that as a good sign to continue with her plans, she ordered breakfast and set out for OfficeMax. She found a small portable printer, raffle tickets, paper, and envelopes.

Back at the hotel, Elsa printed an official form of what the winner receives when he or she gets first prize, which would be an all-expense-paid trip to the tropical island Pharderma. Second prize would be

$3,000. Third prize was a $500 Macy's gift card. On the raffle tickets, she printed the name Pharderma Baptiste Church, on the envelope Pharderma Baptiste Church, 225 Murdock Drive, Charlestown Pharderma, 11318.

Elsa sat back and marveled at her handiwork; if she could pull this off, oh boy, she was good, but she wasn't ready to pat herself on the back yet. Everything had to work, and a lot of the plan would be left to what Elsa started to call the unknown. Forces beyond Elsa were working with her, and she didn't question it; she just rolled with it.

Now it was time to figure out what she would wear for Jartine's event. What would she wear? Elsa absolutely loved getting dressed up. Fashion came so naturally to her, just like breathing. She pulled out four different outfits. What was she in the mood for? High-fashion look, flirty look, sexy, or a little on the conservative side—which one would do? Looking at the four dresses she brought for the occasion, she thought what jewelry she would wear. That would be the deciding factor on the dress. Since everything she was doing was about Sabrina and the purple shoes, she figured, *Yes, I will wear amethyst,* and she had the most beautiful purple amethyst flower pendant.

She tried it on, and it was magnificent. Well, with that, she decided on a simple black tube-top dress with a side slit and some black strappy sandals. She put the ensemble aside and prayed that tomorrow she wouldn't change her mind.

Now for the disguise for Sunday, Elsa pulled out three wigs—one short black wavy one, one curly medium length, and one very long one—a very padded bra, and some underwear with extra cushion on the rear. She tried on everything and finally chose the short wig for the Sunday look. With the bra and underwear, she looked very matronly, not like herself at all. This was perfect, exactly what she was aiming for. With all the details done, she could relax a bit. With all the planning she was doing, she had forgotten to eat, so she ordered a grilled chicken salad with vegetable soup. She had to look good in that tube-top dress. After eating, she suddenly felt so tired; all this excitement was exhausting. Her phone rang; it was Jartine asking if she wanted to have a cocktail with her. Elsa was just so tired and declined, explaining that she had been sightseeing all day. Jartine complained a little but left it alone.

Exhausted, Elsa went to take a shower to get ready for bed. As soon as her head hit the pillow, she was out. She dreamed the two girls together, Sabrina and Briana. They were holding hands, running, laughing; and every once in a while, they would just hug each other, and she saw Brigitte smiling, happiness in her eyes, realizing it wasn't only the girls that were complete; their mom was also. Elsa woke up, and all doubts and fears were wiped out; she knew she was doing the right thing.

Elsa arrived at Jartine's event about a half hour late. For some reason, she had forgotten to take traffic into consideration. Well, nevertheless, she was here. Elsa glanced at herself in the mirror. Wow, she looked fantastic, and the neckpiece was beautiful! Elsa had an unnatural love for jewelry, not just precious gems; she loved everything except plastic.

Jartine appeared, it seemed, out of nowhere, looking absolutely fabulous in a red fitted gown with one shoulder exposed, and her hair was in an upsweep hairstyle with lovely curled loose hair on her neck. She had certainly filled in since college; back then, she was close to anorexic. Looking at her now, she realized Jartine had come a long way. Feeling so much pride, Elsa hugged Jartine tight and told her how proud she was of her.

Jartine told Elsa, "I am telling you now that necklace has to stay here with me. I believe you owe me a gift for my achievements, and that necklace is my gift."

Elsa just laughed. One thing she never did was give her jewelry away especially since each piece was made by commission or a gift from her husband. No, Jartine will get a lovely gift—just not this one—and this particular piece was a gift from her husband for her fortieth birthday.

Jartine knew Elsa, and she replied, "Elsa, even back in college, you had a collection. One less piece wouldn't hurt you."

"Jartine, I love you like a sister, but if you are serious, the answer is no. If you are not, well, still the same answer—no."

Interlocking elbows with Elsa, Jartine mentioned, "You can't expect a girl not to try. Well, I want you to meet someone."

As Elsa turned, there stood an Adonis of a man, the pure definition of tall, dark, and handsome. He had a strong face with a square jawline, full lips, a broad nose, almond-shaped eyes, eyelashes longer than her own, and his hair was cut very low. Wow!

"Elsa, meet Galent. Galent, this is my best friend from back in the day. Elsa, Galent is a comedian."

"Ah, wonderful. Are you performing this evening?"

"No. I'm here just supporting my girl. Have you read her book?"

"Actually, I have not."

"Well, I happen to have a copy right here. The title of the book is *A Black Woman Uncensored* by Jartine Abacourt."

"Hmmm, this looks like an interesting read, Jartine. Thank you, Galent."

Someone was on the microphone, saying, "Ladies and gentlemen, can we be quiet for a moment? My name is Michael Harart, and today we are here to honor my best client yet. She's a strong African American woman, and we must understand this is her first book. As her public relations person, I tell you now there will be more to come. Please, everyone, stand up for my girl, Jartine Abacourt."

Jartine walked up to the platform with an air of confidence.

Elsa spotted Ophelia, Jartine's daughter; she was crying. As a Black woman, Elsa felt so much pride. In her mind, she thought, *We as Black people have gone through so much. Little by little, the world will see us shine.*

Jartine accepted the trophy. "First, I want to thank God because without him, this would not be possible. Thank you, Ophelia, for putting up with me, and thank you, Galent, for telling me that I can do this. Thank you to my fans that made this book a bestseller."

Elsa thought, *Yep, I have got to read this book, and when I get back, I will send her a gift of congratulations, a nice piece made just for her.*

After two hours of festivities, talking, eating, and drinking, Elsa was ready to call it a night; she had a bigger day ahead of her.

After she showered and pampered herself, Elsa took out the purple shoes. She had to find out what time they would be leaving for the mall. One shoe in each hand, she just thought of Sabrina, and she was there. Sabrina was sleeping. Wow, this little girl slept funny; she was on her face, her knees were tucked under her stomach, and her buttocks was in the air. It didn't look comfortable at all. Elsa heard people talking. She found everybody else in the house in the living room. All Elsa wanted to know was what time they would be leaving for the mall. At the same moment, Brigitte asked Carmele that same question.

Elsa wondered, *Was that a coincidence, or did that happen because this is what I just thought?*

Wow, the stones had more power than she thought.

Hmmm, let me see...what airline, flight, and time was Myrtho, Brigitte, and Sabrina going to be on?

Charlie turned to his mom and asked, "What time is your flight, plane number, and gate?"

Myrtho seemed frustrated with Charlie. "How many times are you going to ask me the same question? You just asked me that fifteen minutes ago."

Charlie said, "I don't know. I forgot. Sorry. Just tell me again this time. I will write it down."

"The airline is Pan Am, flight time is eight thirty, flight number 747, and it is gate number seven."

Carmele said to Brigitte, "I wanted to go to church tomorrow before taking you to the mall."

Brigitte asked, "So what time are you going to church?"

Carmele answered, "At 11:00 a.m."

Elsa thought, *That's cutting it real close. People in America have to be at the airport at least two hours before their flight, and they lived an hour away from the airport.*

Brigitte replied to Carmele, "Can we go to the early Mass? That's cutting it too close with the amount of things we need to do tomorrow. Remember, we have to be at the airport by 6:30 p.m."

Elsa thought, *Yes, that sounded much better.*

Carmele said, "OK, we can do that so we can be at the mall by noon."

Great, Elsa got her time, but she still wanted to test the stones' power. Elsa saw the dishes were full and thought Joshua should do it.

Joshua was on the computer, playing a video game. He got up and said, "I'm going to do the dishes."

Elsa couldn't believe it. She said, "OK, last time." She thought Brigitte should make breakfast for everybody before church.

Just then, Brigitte says, "You know, I'm going to make breakfast for everybody before church."

Carmele said, "Really! Oh, that's great! All I have to do is get the kids ready. Oh, thanks, Brigitte. Thank you very much."

Meanwhile, Joshua was in the kitchen, wondering what on earth made him want to wash the dishes. He was in the middle of a battle with his cousin Vladimir, and he was winning; he didn't get it. Well, he's here doing it; might as well get it over with.

Brigitte was trying to figure out if she had just lost her mind. Why would she offer to make breakfast for everybody? Now she was stuck; she had to wake up early.

Elsa, on the other hand, was having a ball. She said, "One more time." She thought Charlie should give his wife a kiss on the left cheek. Charlie got up and gave Carmele a kiss on the left cheek.

Carmele said, "What was that for?"

Elsa thought, *Because I love you.*Charlie said to Carmele, "Because I love you."

Carmele said, "I love you too, Charlie. I feel like it's my birthday—Joshua's doing the dishes without being told, Brigitte is going to make breakfast. It couldn't get any better than this."

Elsa thought that Charlie should get both boys, Luke and Manny, ready for church in the morning, and Charlie said, "Carmele, you get a little extra sleep tomorrow. I'll get the boys ready for church."

Carmele said, "OK. I'm convinced it must my birthday or I'm dreaming." Pinching herself, she stated, "Nope, I am awake. Well, I'm going to bed...just in case this is some sort of joke. Good night, everyone, and thank you."

Charlie was thinking, *Why did I just say that? I don't even know. Now I have to get up early to get Luke and Manny ready.*

Brigitte and Charlie looked at each other, both of them thinking the same thing: *We are having mind lapses.*

Thinking her job is done in the Baptiste household—*wham*—she was back at the hotel room. Her phone was ringing.

"Hello, baby. Where were you? I've been calling for one hour now."

"Darling, I had a few drinks this evening at the event, and when I got back, I fell asleep."

"Oh, OK. What time is your flight tomorrow?"

She had not booked the flight back home yet, so she said her flight was at eight thirty and she would be stopping in New York to get a connecting flight home.

"Well, why didn't you get a straight flight home?"

Elsa said that she wanted to do some shopping in New York.

Yep, that's his wife—shopping was her favorite thing. "OK, darling, call me when you know what time you are to arrive home so I can pick you up."

"OK, love. Go back to sleep."

Elsa had both shoes in one hand; with the other hand, she called the airport for Pan Am flight 747 at 8:30 p.m. The operator started to tell her that the flight was booked, and suddenly she said, "Oh, madam (madam again—Elsa hated being called madam), a spot just opened up. It's in middle class."

"That's fine. I will take it." Putting the phone down, she dropped to her knees. Holding the shoes together, she started to pray,

"God, hi, it's me. OK, God, it seems you have put a supreme power in my hands. God, the power of these stones is greater than I ever anticipated. I can control a person's thoughts. I can be somewhere else in a room, and no one is aware of my presence. God, I don't know what else these stones can do, but one thing I know is no one else must know about the power of these stones...and, God, I am about to give these shoes to an eight-year-old little girl. This is crazy, God, so what I'm asking from you"—she held each shoe up in the air—"God, whatever happens to Sabrina with the shoes, whoever she tells about the shoes, no one must believe her, and if it all goes the way it should, Briana must know in her heart that she must tell no one but me about what has happened to her. God, she must know to come to me. God, when these stones leave me, you must guide Sabrina and keep her safe from harm. In Jesus's name, amen."

Getting up, Elsa felt a total wash sweeping over her body, a cleansing from the inside; her mind felt free, no worries existed, no second-guessing, just a complete feeling of pure bliss.

The sun filled the room with a warm glow. Elsa woke up. She was refreshed, and her soul felt free; the heaviness she had been carrying for the last eight years was gone. The shower felt better. Her breakfast was the best she had ever had. The love she felt inside was toward everything—the air, the planet—everything was more beautiful than ever.

Now to begin putting on the costume for the day—first the padded bra, padded panties, with a wrap dress. She took a look at herself in the full-length mirror, and she was like, *Wow, I am supposed to look matronly, yet I look amazing! Instead, I look voluptuous, it's boom bam! So this is what a curvy woman feels like. I can definitely get used to this.*

She tried on the short wig, Nah, it didn't do anything. She tried the long wig, which went down to her waist. In the mirror, she looked like a cartoon character, *boom bam* everywhere; her mind kept repeating the words *boom bam!* Elsa seemed to be having a bit too much fun with herself.

OK, what to do with her face? She still looked like herself. Being brown skinned, that didn't leave too much she could do, so she decided to go darker. By the time she was done, she was ebony. Looking at herself in the mirror, she couldn't quite describe what she looked like—dark as night, body like a mermaid, and hair down to her waist. She didn't look real. Well, it's the year 2008. Plastic surgery is a multibillion-dollar industry; almost everyone had fake hair, fake nails. She would fit right in.

Even though nothing at that moment felt real, her mind started to go to the what-ifs. She refused to let them in. It was time to go. One last look in the mirror. *Wow, boom bam!*

She arrived at the mall at precisely 11:30 a.m. She wanted to know what time they would arrive. She was in the car with Carmele, holding the shoes in her hand.

Myrtho just asked, "Carmele, are we there yet?"

"Mommy, we should be there in about ten minutes—there is no traffic."

Myrtho said, "OK, good. You know, Carmele, I get excited for everything."

"I know, Mommy."

Smiling, Elsa was back in her car. She had ten minutes. She walked into Manny's Children's Shoes. The store attendants were busy with customers. The cashier was busy, and no one noticed her walk in. She walked to the far end of the store; no one was there. She took both shoes again and thought everyone in the store should ignore her and the cashier should do whatever Elsa wished, and after she leaves with Sabrina, Myrtho, and Carmele, no one in the store should remember them ever being there.

Holding the shoes, she thought, *These shoes will be the only thing that Sabrina will see or want.*

Taking the shoes to the front glass window, she set one in the glass case. She put it right in the middle and moved all the other pretty shoes away from it; she wasn't taking any chances. Waiting, she spotted Sabrina walking toward the store. Her heart started to beat faster than ever before; in fact, she felt that other people can hear her heart beat—no way anything could be this loud and no one can hear it. Wait, she did say that everyone was to ignore her. OK, everything will work out.

Brigitte was telling her mom, "Mommy, I'll meet you back at the car. Sabrina and I are just going to walk around the mall. Call me when you're done."

From where Sabrina was standing, she could see something sparkling in the store ahead; she wanted to see what it was. Pulling her mommy toward the sparkling thing, she had to see what it was. As soon as Sabrina saw what was sparkling, she screamed, "Mommy, Mommy, do you see that shoe?"

"What shoe! What shoe, baby?"

"The purple shoes, Mommy!"

Brigitte looked and saw what Sabrina was pointing at. It was a patent leather shoe, deep purple with a jewel center and butterfly wings; it looked expensive—very expensive. Sabrina was actually pulling her in the store. Brigitte didn't want to go in this store. She stopped Sabrina and said, "Darling, we don't need to go in this store."

Sabrina looked as if she would cry and said, "Please, please, please, Mommy, please."

"Darling, I only have twenty dollars on me, and those shoes look very expensive."

Sabrina started with the "Please, please, please, Mommy, I just want to look at them." Just then, the salesperson came inside the window display and put a sale sign on the purple shoes. Sabrina screamed, "Mommy, Mommy, did you see that? The shoes are on sale."

Brigitte thought, *No way I can afford those shoes,* and Sabrina looked close to tears.

"OK, baby, we will go in, but remember I only have twenty dollars on me."

As they walked in, the same salesperson that had put the For Sale sign on the shoes came toward them. She was a very voluptuous woman, a very dark pretty woman with a sparkle in her eyes, just like the sparkle in the shoes.

Brigitte thought, *What an interesting-looking woman.*

Sabrina said, "Can I please try on this shoe?"

Elsa asked her what her size was, and Sabrina said size eight.

"Well, I am so sorry, dear, we only have that one shoe left, and it's a size seven."

Sabrina said, "Please can I try it on?"

"Of course, my dear."

Meanwhile, no one in the store was paying Elsa and her customers any mind. Elsa was amazed. She went to where she had hid the box with the other shoe and brought it to Sabrina. She already knew the shoe would fit; her investigator had informed her Sabrina's shoe size already. The shoes were made for Sabrina. She slid the shoe on Sabrina's foot; it was a perfect fit. They finally had a home, and they looked magnificent on this beautiful child's foot. Sabrina was beyond excited. Elsa looked at Brigitte, and she just looked depressed.

Sabrina said, "Can I try both shoes on?"

"Of course, sweetheart." Going to the front window, she grabbed the other shoe and put them on Sabrina.

Sabrina screamed, "Oh my god, Mommy, look at these shoes! Mommy, I feel like a princess!" Sabrina looked at Elsa and said, "I never want to take these shoes off ever. Oh my god, I feel amazing!"

Elsa looked at Brigitte. She said, "Can I wrap this up for you?"

"Wait, how much are these shoes?"

"They are on sale for ten dollars."

Brigitte was saying, *Wow,* in her head, and Sabrina had this pleading look on her face, so she said, "Yes, please wrap it up."

Sabrina reluctantly took off the shoes and gave them to Elsa, holding the shoes for a slight moment before placing them in the box.

Elsa thought, *The cashier should get away from the register right about now.*

"Please come to the cashier with me so I may ring you up."

At the cashier, Elsa mentioned to Brigitte that today, and today only, they are having a raffle giveaway for anyone that buys shoes today, and would she like to enter.Brigitte said, "Really, and what are the prizes?"

"Well, the first prize is a dream trip vacation, second prize is cash, third prize is a gift certificate for a popular store."

Brigitte mentioned that she doesn't live in the area and maybe it wouldn't be a good idea to be part of the raffle, and Elsa mentioned that the prizes are for locals and nonlocals.

Brigitte said, "Sure."

Elsa proceeded to give her the raffle ticket and asked Brigitte to fill it out.

While Brigitte was filling out the raffle, Elsa looked at the cash register; it was one of those new models that she never saw before, and she hadn't factored this in.

Opening the box, she laid her hands on the shoes and thought, *The cashier should come back right about now, and once Brigitte pays for the shoes, Sabrina should insist on wearing them out.*

She wrote "$10" on a piece of paper. When the casher came back, Elsa gave her the paper, and just then, Brigitte had finished writing all her information on the raffle.

The cashier told Brigitte, "Miss, your balance is ten dollars, please.

Will you be paying cash or credit?"

Brigitte said, "Cash," and gave the cashier twenty dollars, and the cashier returned her ten dollars change.

As soon as the transaction was made, Sabrina asked her mom if she could wear the shoes now.

Brigitte said, "No, dear. These shoes are for going out."

Sabrina said, "Please, Mommy, please," and she put her best pleading face on.

Brigitte was like, "OK, you can wear them now."

Sabrina screamed with glee, and Elsa said, "Sit down, dear. Let me put it on for you?"

Sabrina sat down. As Elsa took the shoes in her hand, she thought, *Sabrina is to only wear these shoes until everything is done.* She put the shoes on Sabrina and said a silent prayer: *God, please let everything go right with this crazy plan I have.*

When the shoes were on Sabrina for the second time, this time Sabrina looked at Elsa with knowing eyes; Elsa knew Sabrina felt something different now.

Elsa said, "Wear these in good health." She walked them to the front and waved goodbye.

Five minutes later, she was in her car on the way back to the hotel. She had to hurry up and take all this makeup off to get ready for her flight. As soon as she was in her room, she dropped to her knees. *God, it's in your hands now.*

On the plane, Elsa could see Sabrina, Brigitte, and Myrtho. They were seated three rows ahead of her. She could hear their conversations clearly. Myrtho was telling Brigitte she didn't understand why she bought such an extravagant shoes for Sabrina.

"Those shoes are for weddings and parties, not for every day."

Brigitte was getting tired. "Mommy, please! Don't you see how happy the purple shoes make her?"

Myrtho rolled her eyes and let out a sigh.

"Sabrina, why you wearing these shoes now? There is no wedding or party going on right now. Take those shoes off. I have your sneakers in my carry-on."

Sabrina said, "Grandma, you don't understand. I feel different with the shoes on. I can't explain it. I just have to wear these shoes."

Myrtho just shook her head and mumbled something in French to herself.

Elsa smiled. *So far so good.*

*****

In New York, Elsa booked her flight to Pharderma for the next evening, deciding she would stay at a fancy hotel for one night and do some shopping before her flight. She wanted to pick up gifts for her kids and husband.

She arrived at the airport at 6:00 p.m.; her flight was for 8:00 p.m. As she was going to thorough customs and everything you have to do on an international flight, all Elsa could think about was Sabrina. *What was she doing right now? How was she? Was Grandma still trying to get her to take off the shoes?*—all these questions.

Finally seated, the weight of everything she had just done suddenly made her so tired; her mind and body felt so heavy. Elsa fell into a deep, dreamless sleep. The loudspeaker was announcing, "You must please attach your seat belt."

Again, Elsa looked down. Same thing like the flight coming in; she had never taken the seat belt off again. What was it with these Concord planes?

*****

Paulo was there to pick her up. Elsa was surprised he hadn't sent the chauffeur. She knew her husband's work schedule; he was always busy. Boy, he looked so good. She hadn't realized how much she had missed him. She hugged him. He smelled so good; he always smelled amazing.

"You had a good time, love?"

"Yep, I'm so proud of Jartine. I have a copy of her book. Would you like to read it?"

"Yes, of course, I want to read it. Why did Jartine move to America?"

"Well, remember, darling, she had met an American touring here and fell head over heels for him, and he convinced her to return to America with him."

"Oh, yes, I had forgotten. Is she still with him?"

"No, that relationship lasted only one year, but you should see her daughter. She looks like a model. She's tall and stunning."

Paulo asked, "Is Jartine still skinny?"

"Nope, she has definitely filled out in all the right places."

"Well, I'm happy you got to see your friend and that she's doing well, but I did miss you even though it was only for four days."

"Oh, that is so sweet."

"Yeah, every once in a while, I have to show you my sweet side."

Suddenly Elsa woke up out of her trance just to realize that she had been sitting in the bed, remembering the past events that lead to now, right now. So far, everything she had done has worked; the plan was unfolding very well. Now she would see both girls together for the first time. She had to remember not to cry. What would she say or do?

CHAPTER TEN

Packing her overnight bag, she heard her husband come home.

She went to greet him. "Hello, darling."

"Love, tonight I will be sleeping at my sister's."

Paulo was flabbergasted. "Why?"

"Well, Briana needs me."

"Why?"

"Darling, she's my goddaughter, OK? Please, love, it's only one night. I'll be back tomorrow."

"Briana has a mother. Why do you need to go?"

"Well, sweetie, I think sometimes it's hard for Briana to speak to her mom because she sees that her mom is always busy, being a queen and all."

"So your kids don't need you?"

"Love, my kids are older, and they are very self-reliant...plus they have you."

*****

Briana had heard the door to the front open, and she came to see who was home. Seeing her uncle, she ran and jumped on him. He was laughing and gave her a bear hug and kiss.

"Uncle, Auntie is sleeping over tonight in my room."

"Why your room? The castle has many rooms."

"Oh, I want her to sleep in my room. My bed is huge."

"Well, so when are you leaving?"

"The chauffeur is picking us up at seven this evening."

"Well then, finish packing. Don't forget anything that you will need."

In the limousine, Briana held her godmother's hand the whole way. Elsa was in her own world, she hadn't visited the castle in more than eight years. Upon her arrival, Queen Gitte was at the door to greet her.

"Oh my god, you are here. You never come here."

"No, I was here for the ball, remember?"

Gitte said, "That doesn't count. The whole country was here." She interlocked her arms with her sister's and daughter's and said, "When I heard you were sleeping over, I had the cook make your favorite dessert."

On the dining room great table was a huge dish of warm bread pudding with liquor sauce. Elsa hadn't had that for a long time; no one made it better than her auntie Gladen, but Auntie stopped baking ever since her feet operation.

Just then, Gitte said, "Guess what—Auntie Gladen had given me her famous recipe."

Elsa's mouth started to water. Thank God she had forgotten to eat at home. One bite of this amazing bread pudding sent Elsa back to her childhood and the days she spent with her wonderful auntie, closing her eyes to savor this wonderful treat.

Gitte was saying, "This is so delicious."

Elsa opened her eyes and said, "You have to save some of this for me to take home tomorrow."

Gitte said, "Of course. I'll have the cook put your portion away now."

"Well, Gitte, I've had a long day. Thank you for this delicious treat. I need to turn in now."

"Which room do you want to sleep in?"

"If it's OK with you, Briana wants me to sleep in her room."

"Elsa, are you sure? This castle is huge. We have complete apartments in here."

"Mommy, please, I want Auntie Elsa to sleep in my room."

"Well, OK, no problem."

Briana's bathroom was amazing. Elsa loved the castle bathrooms. Briana had a huge stand-up shower that sprayed water from three sides. You don't have to change knobs; you just say out loud, "Warm water," "Cold water," or "Hot water." Whatever you say, you get. The bathroom had a Jacuzzi, which had three steps to come up to it, and it was big enough for six adult-size people.

After showering, she decided she had to tell her husband about this amazing shower, that they had to get one because all her muscles felt completely relaxed. Both of them bathed and were ready for bed. Briana asked her auntie to read to her.

"What would you like me to read to you?"

"Anything, Auntie."

Briana had an impressive selection of books for such a young child. Elsa pulled out *The Multiple Faces of Jean Paul* by Tahisa Limage.

That book looked interesting.

"Briana, have you read this one yet?"

"No. My tutor just had three boxes of books delivered to me last week."

"OK. This one sounds good."

Just as Elsa opened the book, there was a soft knock at the door. Briana opened the door, and it was Sabrina, looking exactly like Briana. Sabrina saw Elsa, and she stood agape for a moment.

"Oh my god, you look like my auntie Elsie!"

"Well, Sabrina, please meet my auntie Elsa, who is also my godmother."

"Wow, this is too much!" Sabrina exclaimed.

Briana started to babble. "I went to my auntie's house today and told her everything, and she wanted to meet you, so she's sleeping over."

Sabrina started to say, "You look like me. Your auntie looks like my auntie. How is this possible?"

Auntie Elsa explained, "Well, darling, you see, there are millions and millions of people on this earth, so God just couldn't think up so many different faces, so everybody has a twin in the world."

"OK, I accept that, but can you explain why Briana found someone to believe her and no one...I mean not even my mom...believes anything I say. They all think I have this great imagination. I couldn't make this stuff up if I tried."

Elsa answered, "Well, I don't know. So, dear, tell me, how have you come to us?"

Sabrina replied, "Well, ever since I got these purple shoes, I have been able to come here, always here, never anyplace else."

"Hmmm," Elsa replied. "So it seems the key is the shoes. When you go to sleep, where are the shoes?"

"Well, they are right next to me. I want to see them, so I place them on my night table by my bed."

"Well, tomorrow night, can you go to sleep with the shoes on?"

"How is that possible? This is a dream. I am dreaming. What good would wearing the shoes do if I am sleeping and this is all a dream?"

"Well, my dear, why don't we just have an experiment and you just wear them to bed?"

"OK, I will put—"

*****

Shaking, shaking again; she was being shaken.

"Sabrina, wake up. You have to get ready for school."

"Mommy, my dreams are continuing!"

"Oh, Sabrina!" Brigitte exclaimed. "I don't have time for this now. I am late. You are late. Come on, we have to hurry up."

Sabrina didn't get it; no one would listen to her. *Why did Briana's aunt Elsa listen to her?* Questions, questions, so many questions.

It seems she was in this one alone; this made her a little sad. "OK, Mommy, I'm up."

"You want me to pick your clothes out?"

"No, no, Mommy. I'm not a little girl anymore. I know what I want to wear."Brigitte, always amazed at how grown Sabrina was, shook her head and replied, "OK. So hurry up, love. We need to be out of here."

CHAPTER ELEVEN

Meanwhile, Elsa and Briana woke up late that morning. They had stayed up late just talking. Briana was so full of questions, and Elsa told her that in due time, all her questions will be answered. That seemed to satisfy the child. The castle had a full-equipped gym with trainers, plus they had the workout clothes there for you. Awesome! Elsa had packed some sneakers and headed straight for the gym. She worked out hard, and it seems that her body needed to exert so much energy. She trained as if she was going in a competition.

After working out, she headed back to Briana's bedroom for that fabulous shower system she had. Every muscle in her body felt alive and wonderful; she so needed this shower system at her home. After the shower, starvation set in. There was a wonderful smell emitting from the castle kitchen. Elsa just followed her nose. They had set up everything on the dining room table—fruits of all types, croissants, ham, eggs, a smorgasbord of food—it all looked amazing, and she sat down and ate with relish. Finally, Queen Gitte showed up and joined her for breakfast and they chatted and Gitte asked if she was leaving today. Elsa replied that she was going to stay for one more night.

Having just seen Briana earlier with her tutors, she was so happy her daughter was all smiles and in a happy mood. She guessed her sister had something to do with her daughter's smiling face, so the fact that Elsa was staying another night pleased Gitte so much—anything to see her little girl happy and not withdrawn. Lately she was extremely worried about her daughter's mood swings.

Suddenly King Sigor showed up, looking at Elsa with open hostility. "What are you doing here?"

Gitte was taken aback by her husband's cruel tone with her sister. Elsa ignored Sigor as if it was only she and Gitte in the room; he wasn't worth a reply. Gitte noticed that too, yet she decided to calm her husband down first; she would deal with Elsa later. Taking him by the arm and whispering in his ear, she consoled him and told him, "Darling, please, she's my sister and our daughter's godmother, and, believe it or not, Briana is smiling again, and I believe it's all Elsa's doing, so please be cordial to my sister. When was the last time she came to visit us? I cannot even recall."

Sigor's mind was blowing up. "How dare she show up here unannounced, and who does she think she is ignoring my question? I am the king! This is my castle!"

He was so infuriated, yet his beautiful wife was speaking sweetly in his ear. He could never deny her anything; she was his life, his air, his weak spot. She was saying how Briana was smiling again. This seemed to have calmed him down, yet his mind was blowing up with red flags. *What was Elsa doing here?* With that, he kissed Gitte on the forehead and walked away, yet before he did, he made eye signals to the guard to keep close watch on Elsa. He didn't trust her at all.

While eating, Gitte questioned Elsa on her behavior when the king had asked her a question. "Why did you not reply to him? You acted as if he wasn't even there. Elsa, he is my husband, and he is the king of Pharderma. You must show more respect."

Elsa told Gitte, "King or no king, you don't come up to me and ask me what I am I doing here. And by the way, whose castle is this anyway? Gitte, it is your castle. He married into your kingdom! Our legacy is here in this castle! Gitte, he is a king, yet you must remember, he is a man first and part of the human race. That being said, you do not speak to me with disrespect and expect me to reply to you! Sorry, Gitte, he had that one coming to him."

"Well, Elsa, you must understand he is the king, and his bark is bigger than his bite."

Elsa just thought, *Little do you know.*

"OK, enough about him. Let's say we go into town...just the two of us."

Gitte, with a deep sigh, replied, "Elsa I am the queen. I just can't go into town like that. When I do go into town, it is planned a week in advance. The places I visit are told I am coming, and there is extra security everywhere. Most of the time the store or restaurant or wherever stays closed to the public while I am there, and that's protocol."

Elsa thanked her lucky stars that she wasn't queen. Not going to places at her own will seemed too much; freedom was priceless. She told Gitte she was boring. "How about I go to town with Briana after her lessons?"

"OK, only if you take security with you. Elsa, Briana is the princess."

With a deep sigh, Elsa agreed to the extra security measures.

CHAPTER TWELVE

The town in Pharderma was beautiful; they called it the Town of Image. There were picturesque buildings and stunning cafés with museums to all your fancies. Pharderma had a rich history, and the people were all proud. You could find the best chocolate here. It seemed the soil was special. Everything in Pharderma was just better, richer, bigger. They went to Rene Chocolate House, which was an outside café, where you found the best cocoa, the best everything. They got a table right outside, under a beautiful palm tree. Elsa asked the guard to please stay in the car to give her and Briana privacy. He agreed as long as he can see them from his position.

Elsa sat with her back to the guard and positioned Briana so that he could see her side only. She didn't know if they could read lips, nor was she taking any chances. They ordered, and the food was beyond delicious, and finished with a chocolate mousse cake and ice cream—so delicious it felt sinful. Keeping the conversation light all through the meal and watching the neighboring restaurateurs to see if anyone recognized Briana—everyone seemed to be engrossed in their own world—also taking her mirror and acting as if she was checking her face, she was keeping watch on the security guard in the car. At one point, she noticed his eyes were closing, so immediately she changed the conversation with Briana and told her about the king's reaction to seeing her at breakfast that morning. Poor Briana looked so confused.

"Auntie, why would my daddy do that?"

"Well, sweetie, your daddy is so jealous of your mommy that maybe he might have been thinking that I would want to go out with her...just like I am doing with you right now."

"Oh, OK, Auntie, I understand. Yes, I know Daddy's really jealous of Mommy."

"So, darling, with that being said, we must assume that your father will station a guard outside your bedroom door tonight. He didn't realize I had slept over last night, yet he knows I am sleeping over tonight."

"Auntie, why would Daddy do that? You're my godmother and my auntie and my mommy's sister?"

"Well, love, your daddy, the king, trusts no one."

"Yes, this is true. I have seen and heard him always telling Mommy she can't go anywhere without her guards."

"All right, love, so you see, we have to do something because if Sabrina just shows up out of thin air, she will be captured. We cannot let that happen, OK? So this is what we are going to do. Tonight you will get all the children that live in the castle to play a game of soccer in the hallway outside your room. This way, when Sabrina shows up, I will hide her, and I'll have one of the kids hit a ball to the guard's head. He'll be temporarily blinded, and we get Sabrina in your room. After that, the guard will be so upset that he will break up the game, which will be fine because Sabrina will already be in the room, safe and sound."

"Wow! Auntie, you are a genius."

Elsa just smiled; she was surprising herself more and more every day.

When they arrived back at the palace, Sabrina and Elsa gathered all the children and told them that before bedtime, they will have a treat, a game of soccer.

One little boy said, "Wow, I love soccer! Why haven't we done this before?"

"Well," Briana said. "It's because my auntie is here. She's my fun aunt, and she thought of this."

Elsa took the little boy to the side and asked him his name. He said his name was Manny.

Elsa said to Manny, "So, Manny, what do you think of all the guards posted all over the castle?" He said the guards scare him. "Well," Elsa said. "Tonight I think the king will post a guard in this hallway."

The boy's smile went away. Elsa noticed it right away.

"Why is your smile now a frown?"

He said that the guards will not let them play a game in the hallway.

"Well, they will if I mention to the queen that we will have game night tonight!"

Immediately his smile came back.

"There's only one thing—can you keep a secret?"

Manny got serious all over again. "I am seven years old. Of course, I can keep a secret!"

"Well, Manny, we want to play a little trick on the guard, yet I need your cooperation to do this."

Immediately his shoulders squared up, and his chin went up. "Anything, Auntie Elsa."

"Well, when I do this sign"—Elsa tagged at her ear—"we will make sure you have the ball at that point, and I want you to purposely aim for the guard's head. Can you do that, Manny?"

"Of course...anything for my favorite girl's auntie."

With that, Elsa hugged Manny tight and watched his face turn red. She then gathered all the children and told them about how the game is going to go, yet only Manny knew why he was supposed to have the ball most of the time. To encourage the kids more, Auntie Elsa said that a couple of hours before the game they would also have movie night with popcorn and candy.

"What movie, Auntie Elsa?"

"Tonight, movie will be *ET the Extra-Terrestrial.*" Yes, all the kids knew about that movie. Auntie Elsa, on the other hand, needed a movie to inspire the children especially Manny.

Now to find Queen Gitte. With Briana, they went to Gitte together, and Briana was excited about movie night and about the soccer game. She was beaming with happiness that all Gitte said was "Make sure you take everything that can break out of the hallway before the game."

Elsa asked Gitte, "Will you be joining us for the movie night and the game?"

Gitte replied, "No. Tonight we have to entertain some businesspeople, yet you two have the best time ever."

"Well, yes, we will." Hand in hand, they walked away. So far, the plan was unfolding without a hitch. Watching them walk away, Queen Gitte shook her head and exclaimed to herself that her older sister never grew up and smiled and walked away to get ready for her guests.

CHAPTER THIRTEEN

The night came. All the children in the castle gathered at the movie theater that the castle had built after Queen Gitte had given birth; it was a gift from the king. It was a grand theater with old-fashioned features and the best sound system money can buy. It could seat one hundred people comfortably and has a popcorn and concession stand—everything to give you the feeling of having a real movie experience. The children were all excited because this was the first time they have ever been allowed inside. It was always for the queen, king, princess, and outside guests, never the children of the people that worked in the castle. Watching the children's faces as they walked in the theater in awe gave Elsa a feeling of pleasure beyond anything; even Briana was beside herself with happiness. All the children, with popcorn and their choice of candy, entered the theater to watch a classic children's tale, *E.T.* Elsa sat with Briana on her right and Manny on her left.

In the meantime, inside the castle near Briana's room, they cleared the hallway of anything that could break because the queen said so. They were all wondering, since when did they ever allow their children to accompany the princess in the movie theater? Not only that, but also the children will be playing soccer in the castle at night? Well, the queen's sister was visiting, and it seemed that whatever she asked of her sister, it was done. Secretly they all appreciated the queen's sister because never before have they seen their children so happy.

After the movie, the kids were all excited (1) because they just saw an amazing movie in style and (2) the night was young; they had a soccer game to play.

Elsa grabbed the soccer ball—they had left one in Briana's room— and said, "OK, kids, it's game time."

The kids noticed with delight that all the hallway furnishings were gone and, for the first time, noticed how large the hallway was. As predicted, a guard was right next to Briana's room. The goalies were set up, and the game began. The children were having a ball. Even the guard was enjoying himself, listening to the children's laughter. They were all excited and happy. Briana's face was priceless; she was enjoying herself. As planned, Sabrina showed up, thank God, when the ball was on the other side of the room because that's what the guard was paying attention to. Elsa hid Sabrina behind an angled wall and made the signal to Manny. Immediately Manny's face lit up, and he kicked the ball straight at the guard's head. The guard's helmet fell of his head, and he was disoriented for just enough time for Elsa to sneak Sabrina in Briana's room. As soon as the guard adjusted himself, he announced, "That's enough! Game over. Everyone to your respected rooms!"

The children said, "Ah, come on, let us finish our game."

He said, "It's late. Time for bed. That is it."

Elsa approached the guard and said, "Let them finish."

"Miss Elsa, with due respect, this game is officially over."

"Well, OK, children, good night. There will be other days." Elsa smiled to herself. *This is art!*

Inside the room, Sabrina and Briana were hugging, and Elsa came and hugged both girls and looked down. Sabrina had the purple shoes on.

"Sabrina, please take your shoes off. I would like to take a look at them."

Sabrina took them off. Elsa thought about the king.

*****

She was in the king and queen's bedroom. The king was telling Gitte, "I am not comfortable with your sister here, and what is she doing here?"

"Darling, we went over this already. Have you not noticed how withdrawn our daughter has become? She is laughing now. She's playing. She's happy. I'm so busy being a queen I don't have time to be a mother. Elsa, on the other hand, has raised three wonderful, strong-minded kids, and obviously she's doing something right. Elsa is what Briana needs now. So you just stop it...stop it right now. Whenever my sister wants to come here, she is always welcome! Unless, of course, my dear husband the king, you wish to try running your own country and leave me to run my country alone?" With her hands on her hips, Queen Gitte was furious, and she meant everything she just said.

The king took his hands and grabbed his head. "OK, love, whatever you say. No matter...I still don't trust her."

"Of course," Gitte replied. News flash: King Sigor trusts no one.

*****

Elsa was back in Briana's room. Both girls were looking at her oddly.

"What? Why are both of you looking at me like that?"

Both girls started to talk at the same time; Elsa couldn't make out anything.

"OK, one person please tell me. I cannot listen to both of you at the same time."

Sabrina said to Briana, "May I?"

Briana just made a gesture with her hand, meaning "go for it."

"Well, one minute you were talking to us, and the next moment you just froze. Yet we knew you were breathing because we took a hand mirror to make sure. I have never seen anyone freeze like that before...have you, Briana?"

Briana just shook her head no.

"Well, Sabrina, I believe you—these shoes have powers."

Sabrina threw her hands up in the air. "Finally, someone believes me."

Elsa then thought of Brigitte. She found her crying on the phone, telling someone that she had just lost her job. Elsa heard her say, "Poppy, it wasn't my fault. They just downsized."

Again, the girls were staring at her.

"You girls stare at me too much."

"Well, you keep freezing...that's strange." They both said that at the same time.

"Well, Sabrina, Briana, you both see that the purple shoes have power. We have to keep this a secret between us three. Girls, let's hold hands. I am going to hold a shoe in each hand, and each girl hold on to my wrist. We are going to pray because it says in the Bible when three or more pray, God hears it right away. So let's get on our knees."

With a shoe in each hand and Sabrina on her right and Briana on her left, Elsa began to pray. "God, in each hand I hold the purple shoes, and I am with Sabrina and Briana. Each of us know the power of the purple shoes. We must keep this a secret among us because in the wrong hands, the power can be misused. God, help us keep our tongue tight. In Jesus's name we pray, amen."

Each girl repeated the word *amen*."Sabrina, put your shoes back on."

CHAPTER FOURTEEN

The shaking again. *Somebody is always shaking me. Ah!* This time, Sabrina woke, and it was OK to keep this secret.

Her mom was saying, "Come on, Sabrina, wake up. It's a school day."

"Mom, I'm awake."

"OK, love. What would you like to wear today?"

"Mom, go on, do what you have to do. I'm a big girl. I can dress myself."

Brigitte was like, "Well, OK, Miss Big Girl. Breakfast is in a few minutes."

Wow, that was close. Sabrina didn't want her mom to see that she had slept with the shoes on; otherwise, she would get so angry and hide the shoes, and that couldn't happen.

Sabrina found her mom and grandmother at the kitchen table. Her grandma Myrtho was telling her mom that she had to start going to church "because only God knows your struggles and only he or she can help."

Brigitte was saying, "Yes, Mommy...yes, Mommy, I know."

Just then, her cell phone rang, and she was asked if this was Brigitte St. Phard.

Brigitte said, "Yes?"

"Well, congratulations. You have won a first-class ticket to Pharderma."

Brigitte said, "What? Where?"

The person replied, "Pharderma is a small island off the coast of Africa. You will be flying the Concord, first class. Everything is inclusive. You just have to bring your passport and get yourself to the airport."

Just then, Brigitte remembered the Manny's Shoe Store in Georgia, the raffle ticket. She took it off her bag, and the address said Pharderma Baptiste Church, Murdock Drive, Charlestown, Pharderma 11318.

"You must bring the child you purchased the shoes for—that is our condition."

"Well, she has school?"

"You wish to forfeit this prize, Miss Brigitte?" the person replied. "You forfeit, you lose a great opportunity to teach your child something about the world firsthand. Also, this is a once-in-a-lifetime opportunity to visit a wonderful country on the other side of the world."

Brigitte replied, "Madam, when do I have to take this trip?"

"You must take the trip before year-end."

Brigitte was ecstatic because Christmas break was coming up. What a nice Christmas she and Sabrina will have on a tropical island. "My daughter has Christmas vacation at the end of this month, December 23 through January 4."

The person replied, "As long as you arrive before year-end, the going-back date doesn't matter. So would you like us to book your flight for December 24?"

Brigitte, on impulse, exclaimed, "Yes, please."

"And the name of the child you will be traveling with?"

"Sabrina St. Phard."

"Her age and birthdate?"

"She is eight years old, and her birth date is March 22, 2000."

"OK. Miss Brigitte, do you have a passport for you and your daughter?"

Brigitte replied, "No, I do not."

"I will book the flight anyway. You have time to get the passports.

What time would you like to leave?"

Brigitte replied, "The evening, please."

"Your flight is booked first class on the Concord for two people—one adult, one child, flight number 069, gate 19, time 5:34 p.m. As a reminder, miss, you cannot board the flight without a passport, so I suggest you get on that right away."

Brigitte exclaimed with excitement, "Well, thank you—what's your name?"

"My name is Miss Claiment Image."

"Wait, miss, what else does this trip include?"

"Miss St. Phard, everyone that participated in the raffle got an envelope explaining the prizes. Please refer to that letter. Will there be any more questions?"

Brigitte said, "No, and thanks."

"Our pleasure. We will meet you in person in Pharderma. Until then, safe travels."

Brigitte couldn't believe it. Her mom was waiting on pins and needles. She had heard the word *trip*, and that was enough. What trip was she going on?

"Mommy, I won a trip to an island called Pharderma."

Myrtho said, "I never heard of that island. Well, nevertheless, am I going too?"

"No, Mom. The trip is just for two people, and I entered the contest because I had bought Sabrina the purple shoes...you remember in Georgia?"

Myrtho exclaimed, "Of course! How can I ever forget the purple shoes? That's all she has ever worn since you purchased them for her. I can't even get her to wear another shoe. By the time she really needs to wear them, like for a wedding or a party, the shoes will be worn out. Ah, well, congratulations. You are going on a vacation."

"Sabrina, are you happy?"

Sabrina's face was pure happiness. She felt so elated; words couldn't describe the feeling inside of her—pure bliss.

CHAPTER FIFTEEN

Meanwhile, in Pharderma, Elsa's maid, Madam Claiment, got off the phone and said, "Miss, did I do well?"

Elsa replied, "You did wonderfully."

Elsa decided it was now time to visit the good doctor. What her investigator had found out was the doctor that delivered Brigitte's children was originally from Pharderma, and he was King Sigor's classmate at the university. They had always remained friends. Even after Dr. Ricardo Lestin went to practice in America ten years ago, Dr. Lestin did not know Brigitte St. Phard was going to have twins; they never heard two heartbeats and never saw two babies in the sonograms. Brigitte was having serious problems. They had wanted to give her an injection to induce labor. Just then, he got an emergency phone call, and they said he had to take the call. Walking out of the room to take the call, King Sigor told the doctor he needed a newborn baby right away; if not, he would do everything in his power to destroy the doctor's practice in America. Just then, a nurse disturbed his conversation and explained that something is wrong, to please come quickly. The doctor told Sigor, "Let me call you back."

Before getting into Brigitte's room, the nurse explained to the doctor, "I am hearing a second heartbeat. The doctor was surprised and he went and checked for himself.

Brigitte was saying, "What is it, doc?"

"Nothing, just checking. Relax." *Yes, two heartbeats. She is carrying twins. Well, I guess the king gets his baby after all.* "Well, Miss St. Phard, we must do an emergency C-section. I will be putting you to sleep. Nurse, please get her to the operating room as soon as possible, and, Mr. St. Phard, we will not be needing your presence in the operating room."

Igor was so happy the doctor said that because he felt he was losing his legs; at any moment, he was afraid he would just faint, so this was good news.

After they wheeled Brigitte out of the room, he called the king and said, "Yes, you will have your child."

In the delivery room, he put Brigitte to sleep and told everyone else in the delivery room to leave and just left the one nurse that had noticed the two heartbeats. He proceeded with an emergency C- section, taking the first little girl out and handing her to the nurse for cleanup and foot and handprint. The other little girl, he took her and cleaned her himself and did the hand and footprints himself. Just then, as he finished swaddling the baby, a soft knock on the door. Two men and woman dressed in hospital attire asked for the infant. He gave her up with the prints. Closing the door with a heavy heart, knowing what he had just done, he turned around, and the nurse, holding the first infant, said, "What have you done?"

Without responding to the nurse, he went and stitched Brigitte up. When he was through, he told the nurse to place the baby in a cubicle. Taking the nurse's arm to the washroom adjacent to the operating room, she questioned him again, "What have you done? Why did you give those men the twin? Why would you do such a thing?"

"Nurse Liz, what you have seen you must forget. If you do not forget this, I will ruin you. I know where you live. I know everything about you. Breathe a word, and I will destroy you."

She held her hands to her mouth, tears running down her face; so much to lose, no husband to rely on, three kids to feed, mortgage to pay—so much to lose. She needed this job; she had worked so hard to become a nurse, her mother's dying wish. She had no choice but to stay quiet.

Elsa's investigator had found that nurse, and he approached her. It didn't take long before she broke down and told him everything. Her tears wear long and hard; she had carried this guilt for eight years.

Elsa told the investigator that she would never be charged and offered her immunity. With a lighter heart and no fear of consequence from the good doctor, she recollected that night as if it had happened yesterday. As promised, Nurse Liz was given a new identity and a new home completely paid for.

CHAPTER SIXTEEN

The Pharderma Baptist Church was founded five years ago by none other than the good doctor Ricardo Lestin. He had given up his practice in America to become a pastor. It was time to pay the good doctor a visit.

Walking in the church with an air of purpose, she asked the church secretary for the pastor; he came.

Elsa asked, "Is there a place we can speak privately?"

The pastor recognized Elsa and said, "Of course. Come this way, please. I have an office back here."

"Thank you, pastor."

"I must say, Sister Elsa, I am surprised of your visit. I haven't seen you in church in years."

"Well, pastor, sometimes I visit other churches, and sometimes I pray at home. There is only one God, correct?"

"Yes, indeed, yet he loves to be praised."

"Understood." (The pastor had no idea what had brought Elsa to him this afternoon; he didn't know she was in the castle the night of March 22, 2000.)

Arriving at his office, he asked Elsa to sit. She sat, and he went behind his impressive desk, folded his hands, and said, "How may I help you?"

"Pastor Lestin, why, may I ask, did you leave your striving career in America to come back to Pharderma?"

Suddenly the pastor, who was very light skinned with curly black hair, a straight regal nose, with hazel eyes, and very good looking, started to change to different shades of pink.

Elsa could feel his anger; it was just below the surface, and he replied that, "I also felt I didn't want to be a doctor any longer and God had called me to do his work."

Elsa smiled and said, "I see. Would guilt have anything at all to do with your decision, my good doctor?"

Pastor Lestin replied, "What are you talking about, Sister Elsa?"

"Well, Dr. Lestin, the night of March 22, 2000—do you remember

this said night? It is the same night my sister gave birth to a stillborn baby girl. How I know is because I buried her. The king gave me my dead niece to bury! I buried her little body right outside my sister's bedroom suite and marked it with flowers that I had purchased for my sister as a birthing gift. You see, the flower was in a pot. I broke the bottom of that pot and placed it right over the burial place. After that, I retreated to my room to mourn my niece and try to figure out what I will tell her in the morning when she awakens and asks for her baby—what would I say? Just as tears were rolling down my face, I heard a baby cry. No one else in the castle was pregnant, just the queen, and a baby was crying not three hours from me burying my niece had gone by. I ran to the sound to find my sister awake, holding a little girl, my sister's face full of love and appreciation for life itself.

"Dr. Ricardo Lestin, I know you delivered Brigitte St. Phard's twin girls. Well, do you remember that nurse you threatened? She has confessed to me about every detail that went on that night."

As Elsa was speaking, she did notice that the good doctor started to actually turn red. At this moment, he looked like a lobster. Elsa wasn't aware that light-skinned people can change to so many shades of color; it was quite amazing, yet she felt no fear toward the doctor. He slammed both fists on this precious desk. Papers went flying; things fell and broke. Elsa was as cool as a cucumber; in fact, she was amused.

"Why do you think I am here? I gave up my doctorate to become a pastor. In

America, I was making millions. The king threatened my life. Did you know that? I had no choice but to do his bidding, and up to five years ago, I couldn't live with that guilt any longer—it was eating at my soul, so I gave it all up and returned to Pharderma. I was losing my mind, wondering around Pharderma. I wanted to be nothing, to do nothing. I didn't want anyone to recognize me, so for a month, I lived in your precious national parks until Pastor Jordan Hass found me and convinced me to come live with him at his church. Remember, Pastor Jordan's church's name is the Sanctuary of the Now, so there I learned to talk to God and to forgive myself, and later I opened this church. I gave back, and I have been giving back for my sins. So just don't walk into my church and start asking me questions."

"First of all, pastor, your story has some serious holes in it. You told me you left your doctorate because God called you—no, you left because you realized you were doing the king's bidding at all times. I am sure that wasn't the first time you did something to that extreme for your king. It just started to eat at your soul and your mind was going, so don't come and tell me God called you, the pastor found you, and you just decided this is a great cover. Listen, I am not here to judge you—that's not my calling. Only God judges.

"What I am here for—listen to me carefully, I will only say this once—is it is time to start paying back big time. This is one thing that I do know you did. Brigitte St. Phard will be arriving to our beautiful island, and you, Pastor Lestin, will tell her everything!"

"Are you crazy, lady? I can't do that. Your king will have me killed."

"Don't worry about the king—leave him to me—plus he doesn't

even know you are in Pharderma. Your king doesn't go to church in town. He built a chapel in the palace and he prays there and he hired his own pastor for that chapel, so he doesn't even know you are here. Just remember, you must tell Brigitte the truth…and, pastor, the truth will set you free, only the truth. Only then will God wipe your slate clean."

With his head down, Pastor Lestin said, "Yes, Elsa, I will do as you wish."

"Pastor, I thank you, and God will bless you."

Leaving the pastor with his head still in his hands, she left and decided to sit in the first pew and pray. Getting down on her knees, she prayed. *God, how am I going to take care of the king? Why did I say that to the pastor? I can't take care of the king. With a dip of his eyebrow, the king could have me wiped out.*

In her silence, she gave into the higher power pulling these strings from the beginning and raised her arms. *OK, God, whatever you say, and I am not here to judge my role in this huge scheme of things. Everything was and is and always will be in your hands. I am your puppet. No, no more questions.*

Getting up and walking toward the door, she spotted the holy water; there were three of them. Cupping some in her hand, she washed her face with it. Then going to the other, she put it on her arms. Still not satisfied, she took more and put it on her hair, thinking about what she was doing,

What, God? I'm taking a bath in your holy water. Well, I need all the protection and help I can get.

With that, she walked out.

CHAPTER SEVENTEEN

Meanwhile, in the castle, the king and queen were going at it; everybody else was pretending they didn't hear anything. Yet with the acoustic of the castle, loud sounds vibrated and echoed; you can hear everything—all the yelling and screaming. The king was livid, and the queen wasn't backing down. Queen Gitte was invited to speak at the Women's Summit in the Democratic Republic of Congo for an event that recognized the achievement of Black women that have made it in the community, and they had invited the queen to speak, and she had said yes without consulting with the king. King Sigor wasn't having it, and the queen felt as if she was a prisoner in her own castle, so she also wasn't backing down. In the meantime, Sabrina was cringing in her study room, listening to it all. She can't hear what her professor was saying; the king's roars were drowning out everything.

In the end, the king told her, "You will not go. You will not disobey me, and my word is law!"

Well, that made the queen even more upset than the king. She told him that in a few minutes, a limousine will be picking her up to bring her to a private jet that will take her to the summit and that she will be gone for a few days. "It's 2008, and you, my dear king, are back in the 1700s. I will go and return when I am good and ready."

So the king yelled, "So what about Briana? Who will take care of Briana?"

The queen said to him, "Briana has three nannies and four personnel professors. Briana will be fine, and if anything, I will call Elsa to come and stay here!"

"What! Call your sister to come to my castle? Over my dead body!"

That scared Gitte a little. The king looked like a crazy person, and she felt Elsa might be in danger if she came here; and if anything happened to Elsa, the king had to deal with Elsa's husband, who would properly try to kill him. There would most likely be a civil war. "No, don't call Elsa. Just go."

Her phone rang. "Queen Gitte, the limousine is here to pick you up.

Should I send someone for your bags?"

"Yes, please."

Just then, a knock on the door, and Gitte opened it and motioned to the boy to take her bags.

The king said, "Boy, you put those bags down right now and get out of here!"

The boy ran out of the room. With that, Gitte grabbed her purse and grabbed two of her bags and told the king she is going and she will be back.

As he watched her move toward the door to leave the room, he stood in disbelief that his wife disobeyed him. His queen disobeyed him. All the things he has ever done were for her, and she dared to do this to him. He is the king!

"Gitte, you touch that door to leave, I promise you I will not be the same person when you come back."

Gitte turned around. With steel in her voice, she turned the knob and said, "Watch me. I will go and I will return, and if you think you will treat me any different from what I am used to, then, my dear king, you will see another side of me." With that, she turned the knob and walked out of their suite and walked out unto the awaiting limousine outside.

The king watched as she stepped inside the limousine and drove away. He was in a rage. He swung his arm, and everything on his desk flew off. He yelled for Markis (his personal assistant), "Bring me Johnny Walker Black! Now!"

"Yes, sir." Markis was terrified. He had never seen his king like this. Two seconds later, the king had his liquor, and he was drinking it like water.

In the meantime, all the workers in the castle decided that they didn't want to be in the same wing as the king, and they all went to the west wing. They took Briana also. Everyone was afraid of the king. Never seeing him like this before, they didn't want to know what he would do. To calm everyone down, they decided that they should all go to the theater and watch a funny movie— anything to distract Briana to make her happy. Markis asked Briana what movie she wished to see, and Briana, close to tears, didn't know and told Markis to please choose for everyone. Markis, always a fan of Whoopi Goldberg, decided that *Sister Act* would be a great uplifting movie. So they gave all the children popcorn and candy and ran the movie. The movie lightened everyone's mood, and even Briana found herself laughing and being happy. For the time being, they all forgot about their angry king.

The king, on the other hand, was talking out loud and getting drunker by the moment.

"Who does she think she is? I say what goes on around here. If it wasn't for me, she would never have a child." He pounded his chest. "I am *King Sigor!* Everyone should obey me! Yes, that means you, my *queen!* You gave birth to a stillborn. It's because of me you have a child. Even after eight years, you still never conceived again...not that I have not *tried!*" The king was screaming to no one.

He saw his image in a mirror, grabbed a vase, and threw it at the mirror, and it broke into a million pieces. His study had magnificent bookshelves. He looked at them. They looked too big to him, and with all his anger and strength, he pushed one huge bookshelf, and it was a domino effect. The whole study was getting destroyed. Standing among the devastation that he had created, still not satisfied, he felt all that he had done for her was not appreciated.

"Yes, I will teach you when you come back that I am king."

He grabbed for more liquor. The bottle was empty. Again, he screamed for Markis. No answer; Markis was with everyone else at the movie theater. He yelled for other people. No one came; everyone was gone.

"I will get my own liquor!" He proceeded to the wine cellar, and on the third step, down he slipped and fell down. When his body hit the bottom, his neck hit the corner of the step, his skull cracked, and the king instantly died!

The next day, no one saw the king. Well, the king's chamber had a fully stocked kitchen, and he had all kinds of snacks. Over his huge bed was a state-of-the-art projector. With his voice, he could command everything in the room. There was a pool room, a study/library, and two offices, one for the king and one for the queen. There were enough provisions to last them for a month, so no one questioned the fact that they didn't see the king. Even Briana thought nothing of it. The night before she had to sneak back to her room; she didn't want Sabrina arriving and not finding her. She hugged Sabrina tightly and begged her to go back; she didn't feel safe with the king acting so crazy. Sabrina had been sad yet wished herself back right away. After Sabrina left, she sneaked back to the west wing. They had placed her in one of her nannies' rooms, and she didn't want them to wake up and not find her.

CHAPTER EIGHTEEN

Queen Gitte was getting the royal treatment in Kinshasa, the capital of the Democratic Republic of Congo. She was staying at Fleuve Congo Hotel. The hotel was the lap of luxury, the food was amazing, and the people here were bending over backward to her. She felt so thankful that the embassy invited her to speak to these beautiful intelligent women, feeling like herself again for once in her life. The king made her feel so suppressed. She resented that feeling, as if she didn't have a mind of her own. In front of her was a piece of blank paper. Her speech. What would she talk about? What could she talk about? What could she possibly tell these women? At that moment, she felt like a fraud; she had nothing to share to motivate these women. A soft knock on her door. She opened it, and the ambassador of Congo stood before her and said, "My queen, are you ready to go? You will be on in exactly one hour. The conference room is here in the hotel. There will be 250 guests, and you will be our first speaker for the night. Would you like me to accompany you to the conference room, my Queen?"

"Please, ambassador, can you give me a few more minutes?"

"Yes, my queen. I will return in one-half hour. Thank you very much."

Staring at the blank piece of paper in front of her, she felt like a hypocrite. What could she tell these accomplished women? These women were doctors, lawyers, judges, authors, business owners, CEOs, actresses; there were even a few women ministers.

Getting down on her knees, she raised her arms to the sky and cried, "God, what am I doing here? What do I have to say to these women? My husband tries to control my every move. He keeps spies on me at all times. My home, the castle, is my jail. What inspirational message can I give these women? God, I came here because I was so flattered that people even really knew I existed...because I don't have a voice in Pharderma. I'm just the pretty face for my country, I hate to admit to that, but yes, I wear a pretty dress and wave at the people. I smile at the dinners yet never offering my opinions. What, God, do I have to say? Well, I am here, and, God, I am your puppet. You give me the words, and I will speak them. Thank you in advance. In Jesus's name I pray, amen."

She sat and waited for the ambassador to return for her. She was wearing a gown of white, with yellow trimming. On her neck, she wore the crown jewels, a white-gold neckpiece with a canary-yellow long diamond drop with matching drop earrings. Her hair was swept up in a beautiful braid that looks exactly like a flower. In her hair, she had stuck diamond pins with the flower design. Her makeup was flawless; the makeup artist sent to her worked on her face just like a painter works on his canvas. Gitte believed that she never looked better than today—that did help to boost her confidence. Suddenly a newfound pride came upon her, and she knew that, yes, she was important, and yes, she had something to say.

Walking on the stage, Gitte saw the women's faces, young and old, all eager to hear her. They came for her. More pride was building up, so she decided she would give them her truth.

"Ladies, my name is Queen Gitte St. Jude. My country's name is Pharderma. It is north of the Atlantic Ocean off the coast of Africa. My country claimed their independence on November 24, 1962. My father was chosen to be king, King Sane DeBaptista. He married my mother, Princess Yrtho Orchard from Madagascar. On June 29, 1997, we lost our dear mother. They had six children. I am the fourth born.

"My siblings are Elsa, Karlie, Sigrid, Keycil, and Bianne. My brother Karlie was trained early to take over our kingdom upon the death of our father. Karlie was sent to the finest schools abroad. When Karlie returned, he told Father that he was not interested in running a country. He wanted to be an entrepreneur. My other brother, Keycil, Father felt, was too young and wild in his ways. Elsa, the eldest, fell in love with a rich merchant's son. Sigrid was intrigued with the medical field. All she wanted to do was to become a doctor. The youngest, Bianne, was a teenager at the time, so, of course, that left me.

"In 1998, Father arranged my marriage to Prince Sigor of the island of Madeira. We were wed on December 29, 1998. I found myself queen earlier than I had expected. My beloved father died on August 3, 1999.

"Well, ladies, this December 29, 2008, marks ten years I have been married, and I must admit I have allowed my husband to suppress me. Decisions about the running of my country have been left completely to my husband. In the beginning, it was OK. In the second year of my marriage, my daughter, Briana, was born on March 22, 2000. Being a doting mother was my priority. Letting my husband run the country was easy. Turning a blind eye on everything was easy. I was a new mom to the most precious little girl, the apple of my eye.

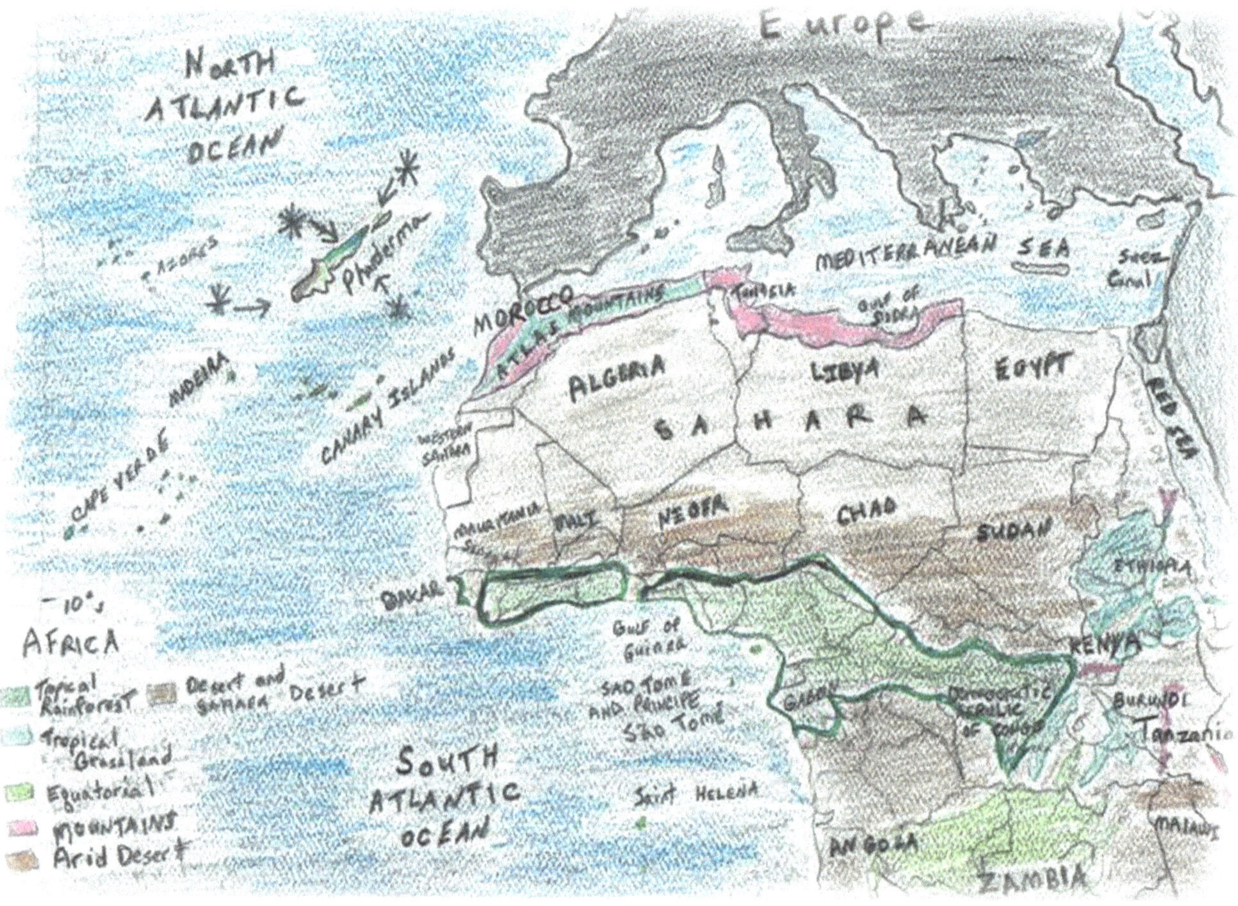

"But, ladies, when I return to Pharderma, I will be returning as the woman that I am, my father's daughter, his choice to run his country. I have a mind. I'm not just someone to greet guests and laugh at stupid jokes.

"My husband, King Sigor, makes it so easy for boys and young men to become anything they want to be, but our women are told they must be good wives, good daughters. In school, they are mainly taught to cook and sew. They are not encouraged to further their education like the boys are.

"I have a daughter. Is that all I want to teach her? No." She shook her head and walked back and forth. The audience was entranced.

"I want my daughter to have every advantage our men do. I want her to be whatever she chooses. Today in America, they have elected their first Black president, Barack Obama, and his wife is a lawyer. I want the future of all women, young and old, to be as promising as they want it to be.

"We need to stand side by side with our men, not walk behind them. The world is changing. We need to flow with the times. You have an opinion, voice it. You want to say no, *say it!*

"So many invitations like this one I have passed up over the years to do just this. Always my husband, the king, said, '*No!* You do not need to go. What do you have to say anyway?' I would feel bad but say nothing and never go.

"This time, when they called for this invitation to speak to you precious women, I was compelled to say yes! Something just clicked inside of me. My king went nuts. Literally, ladies, he went *crazy!* Yet this time I didn't care. How long does another human being control another? Well, ladies, I say, nine years, eleven months, and eight days is enough! I am a woman of sound mind and body. I know what is right and wrong. There is no excuse why I cannot run Pharderma with my husband side by side.

"With that, ladies, I close. God bless every one of you. Continue doing what you are doing, empowering women around the world. They need you more than you know. I need you because of you wanting me here today. I am reborn. Again, God bless you all."

With that, Queen Gitte threw kisses to her crowd and bowed. She felt elated and humbled by these wonderful women. To her ultimate surprise, she got a standing ovation. Pride built up, and so did the tears. The feeling of being loved and accepted as an equal to these women was beyond any other feeling she had ever had. She left the stage with a new inner peace and a knowing that her future as queen of Pharderma will forever be changed; she was ready to face her king.

CHAPTER NINETEEN

The queen's speech was broadcasted on channel 777, and Elsa had watched the whole thing. She was so proud of her little sister. They all had really forgotten this was their country. King Sigor had a way of making you think this was his personal country, not the one he married into. With tears in her eyes, Elsa was so proud; to think her little sister finally grew up. Perfect timing, if ever, considering what was about to happen in the next couple of weeks.

There were reports that the king had never left his chamber, quite unlike him, but no one cared; no one really liked the king.

Returning to Pharderma, Gitte was quiet. She hoped her old submissive self would not return; she prayed for strength. When she arrived at the castle, it was quiet. Her maid Carla informed her that the king has never left his chamber. *Wow,* Gitte thought, *he's not over it yet?* She brought herself up to her full five feet two inches height, held her head up high, and turned the key. No one was there; no king? The bed was never slept on. Confused, she called for Markis.

"Markis, where is the king?"

"My queen, he locked himself in here. We haven't seen him for two days."

The queen replied, "Yet he isn't here."

Markis admitted that after he gave the king the bottle of liquor, they all had decided to leave the king alone. "Since his outburst, no one wanted to bother him, and he is here in the castle because he never left."

Gitte was beginning to get a funny feeling in her gut. "Please, Markis, have everyone help you look. You say he had started to drink?"

"Yes, my queen. He ordered me to bring him a Johnny Walker Black from the cellar."

"Get everyone together, and search the castle."

Not too long after the search, they heard a bloodcurdling scream; it was Carla, and she had found the king's decomposing body at the bottom of the cellar stairwell. The queen made the call to their doctor. Dr. Rafael Colten was summoned. Doctor pronounced the king dead from a broken neck. The general of Pharderma, Gerald Rezau, demanded a complete investigation of his king's death and an autopsy. The advisor, Rudolph Prez, made the announcement on television that the king has died. All over the county, the news spread like wildflower. The country was sad; though he was never liked, he was respected.

Queen Gitte was so sad. She wanted to have a more understanding marriage, the ability to voice her own opinion. Now he was gone, and Briana was fatherless.

Briana wondered why she wasn't sadder; her father had just died, but she wasn't crying. She felt down, but she just couldn't understand why the tears didn't come. *Why am I not crying?* she questioned herself.

Everyone on the small island of Pharderma came to the burial, also from the island the king came from, Madeira. The king's father and mother, King Gordon St. Jude and Queen Alma, Prince Stranoff, and also many other residents of Madeira were there. Prince Stranoff gave the eulogy. It was moving, but the people were quiet; no one except King Sigor's mother, Queen Alma, cried. Queen Gitte hadn't shed a tear; everyone thought she was being strong. She was deeply saddened. When not controlling her, he was a good husband, always with her best interest at heart; she knew he loved her.

King Sigor died on December 7, 2008; he was buried on December 13, 2008.

CHAPTER TWENTY

There was speculation that the queen was to marry King Sigor's brother, Prince Stranoff; even the queen heard the rumors.

She was speaking to Elsa and told her, "Why would I do that to myself—marry another St. Jude? Are there no men left on this earth? Plus, isn't Queen Elizabeth of England ruling without a husband? I am in no hurry." Elsa told her to just heal from her loss.

The prince also heard the same rumors. He thought, *Yes, not denying it, the queen is beautiful,* but over the last ten years, he has come to think of her as a sister. He wouldn't go there; he couldn't go there, plus his own father was getting old; he was the only heir left to the throne.

Meanwhile, Brigitte had requested an emergency passport for her and Sabrina. It came on December 21. Brigitte called the number on the letter to inform them that, yes, she had received it.

The number was Elsa's cell. She disguised her voice and told Brigitte, "Everything is set for your trip. We will see you on December 24."

Brigitte mentioned that Christmas was the next day. "What will we be doing?"

Elsa replied, "My dear prize winner, that, my dear, is a surprise."

There was a lot to do before Brigitte's arrival. Elsa decided the time had come for her to tell her sister the truth. She called Pastor Lestin and informed him she will be picking him up in one hour—that they had to tell the queen the truth.

Pastor said, "OK."

Well, the king was dead now; no one would destroy him or kill him. Elsa called

Gitte and told her she had to speak to her. Gitte wanted to know why. Elsa didn't answer but replied she would be there in two hours.

Elsa arrived with the pastor.

Gitte wondered, *What is he doing here?*

Elsa asked Gitte, "Can we please speak in private?"

Automatically, Gitte's mind went into suspicion mode. What was her sister up to!

They went to Gitte's office. Elsa put her hands on Gitte's shoulders and told her to please sit down. With huge eyes, Gitte sat. Every cell in her body was on full alert, and even her breathing was coming in quick and heavy. Elsa sat in front of her and requested the pastor to sit next to her and told Gitte, "What I am about to tell you will seem false, but I assure you it is all the truth, and I have been carrying this around for eight years."

The story poured out of Elsa like an avalanche. Tears were running down her eyes and cheeks as she told Gitte the whole story—from the moment Gitte's baby was born stillborn until the events that led to this day and what was to come in a few days.

All the while Elsa spoke, Gitte didn't move a muscle; her mind kept screaming, *This isn't true! What is my sister trying to do to me? I have just lost my husband. I have a country to run by myself and a daughter to raise by myself. I don't believe it. It's too incredible. No! I won't believe it!*

Getting up, she looked at Elsa and said to her in a very strong, calming voice, "Elsa, I know you and the king had your differences, yet for you to come here and try to degrade his name is way beyond anything. I would never have expected this of you, my own sister! I don't know why you are also here, pastor, but I think it's time for you and my lovely sister to leave. Leave me alone—now!"

Gitte's whole being was vibrating. Her mind was screaming, *Why, why, why, Elsa, why?*

Elsa knew this was going to happen; that's why she had requested the pastor to be with her.

Getting up, the pastor told Gitte, "My queen, please listen to us. We are not conspiring anything. We are here to tell you the truth. Why would your own sister come up with a story like this? Please sit down and let us finish. My queen, as you know, I am the pastor of the church."

Gitte, frustrated, replied, "Yes, I know who you are. Why are you here?"

"Well, my Queen, I have not always been a pastor. Eight years ago, I was a doctor in America with a thriving practice. King Sigor and I went to the same university in England. We were roommates. Even after the university, we had always kept in touch. He was my friend. In fact, when I wanted to start my practice, I was short on money, a lot of it, and I called him, and he gave me the money I needed to start my practice, and he told me it was a gift. So it was because of him I even had my practice. So when your husband called me on March 22, 2000, he said he wanted a baby and he needed one now, and it so happened that a woman had just given birth to twins, but we never knew that she was carrying twins, and neither did she. So, you see, it was easy to do as he had requested. The mother had been given a C-section. She didn't know she had just delivered twins. Only I knew and the nurse with me. The nurse was busy cleaning up the first baby. So, you see, it was easy to give them the baby girl. As soon as I had footprinted her and filled out the paperwork, there was a knock on the door. Three people came to get the little baby—two men and a woman. As I closed the door after giving them the baby, the nurse had returned, and she went straight to look in on the babies. She came back to me and said, 'Where is the other baby?'

"I told her there is no other baby. She said, 'Doctor, I was there. This woman gave birth to twins, and they were both healthy!' I grabbed her shoulders and looked in her eyes and told her if she was to ever bring up this other baby again, I would fire her and I would make sure she never worked again, not even as a store clerk. I told her as of that moment, she was head nurse, with a $20,000 raise and $10,000 raise every year after that. I knew her home situation. She was raising three kids on her own without any husband. I knew she needed the money. She agreed, and the deal was made."

Gitte started to believe them. She turned to Elsa and said, "If you buried my baby, where is the body?"

For some unknown reason, Elsa knew that one day someone would ask this question. "Right outside your bedroom patio, where the rare purple flowers grow."

Gitte always loved the purple flowers; nowhere else on the island did they grow. A chill went down her spine; she believed them. Thinking about Briana, she could never really get close to her like a mother should, not the way Elsa was close to her three kids. She always thought, *It's because I am a queen. I have a certain status to maintain,* yet deep down inside, something wasn't right, yet she never could know what it was. Also the king never once hugged Briana, never played with her. He knew how to play; she had seen him play with the other children in the castle, never his own. Everything was starting to make sense. She wanted to hate her sister, but she couldn't; the king had threatened her niece and nephews—that was just too much to bear.

She looked at Elsa with tears in her eyes. "May I see the remains of my baby?"

With tears in her eyes, Elsa walked out of the room. She went to the garden shed and found a shovel. With the queen in tow and the pastor, Elsa walked to the beautiful purple flowers, and right in the middle, she had given the queen a beautiful statue of a baby holding a bowl; this was her gift to the queen when the baby was born, and she had told the queen that she knew the perfect spot for it and she had placed it on top of the burial spot. She went and asked the pastor to help her lift it up. After that, she started to dig. Not long, she found the small box she had buried the baby in. She opened the box, and there was the queen's shawl she had used to wrap the infant. Immediately, Gitte recognized the shawl; Elsa had given it to her when she turned twenty-five. It was her most beautiful shawl with its deep-purple color with greens and blues and gold thread entwined and made with the finest silk. She had been looking for it for years. Inside the box was a small plastic; there was a note. Gitte took it and read it. It was in Elsa's hand, dated March 22, 2000.

Here lays Queen Gitte's baby girl. She was stillborn. I am going to call her Amethyst. God, please take care of this baby's soul because I know she had one because she used to beat up Gitte's stomach so bad. Thank you, Lord. Amen.

Gitte was on her knees, crying; her whole body was shaking. She let out the most chilling scream. Elsa and the pastor were also crying. Pastor Lestin picked up Gitte, and Elsa closed the box once more with a silent prayer and returned Princess Amethyst's remains back, placing the statue back in its spot, and didn't even notice that it had taken two people to move it in the first place, all the while tears streaming down her face. Gitte's pain was her pain because she was part of this, and she will fix this.

*****

Back in the study, Gitte had calmed down.

Elsa said, "Gitte, there's more. Do you remember when I went to America with Paulo?"

Gitte, unable to speak, just shook her head yes.

"By accident, I saw a duplicate of Briana. I knew right then that I had found my answer. The king had taken a twin. I hired a private investigator and found everything—the nurse that was in the delivery room." (Elsa neglected to tell Gitte about the purple stones and that Briana had seen Sabrina already; for some reason, the stones had to be kept secret.) Elsa made it seem as if the private investigator had done all the work. "Gitte, Brigitte St. Phard and her daughter, Sabrina, will be arriving here on December 24."

At that remark, Gitte turned three different shades of blue. "Elsa, I cannot give up Briana! I love her with every inch of my soul."

"Gitte, I am not asking you to give up Briana, but please think about it. Brigitte deserves to know she had twins that night, and Briana and Sabrina deserve to know they have each other. Gitte, have you not looked deep inside your daughter's eyes and seen a deep sadness? Why on earth would a princess be so sad? She's only eight years old. Gitte, I believe that twins have a sense that we do not have. Briana doesn't even know why she's so sad. Gitte, I am sure you and Brigitte can come to an understanding. Briana would not be here if it was not for her."

Gitte, looking so tired, replied to Elsa, "OK, I'll think of something.

Does Briana know?"

Elsa had to say, "No, Briana doesn't know" (because in reality, all Briana knew was that Sabrina looked just like her, and that was freaking her out.) "So when they arrive, we will tell them together."

"Elsa, why have you kept this secret from me? You knew about Briana's mother's and sister's existence for six months now."

"Gitte, King Sigor doesn't react well to people that cross him. Do you think I would risk my children's lives? If he could take someone else's child, what could he not do?"

Gitte, looking down at her hands, thought of her strong-minded husband and the way he ruled with an iron fist and the way he controlled their whole marriage, and her last episode caused him to be so angry that he died from that anger. Yes, she understood.

"Elsa, what do you think—I could offer Brigitte St. Phard to live here in the castle? With both girls together, I do need a female advisor."

"Gitte, that's a wonderful idea. The private investigator did mention that Brigitte was currently unemployed and struggling to make ends meet in America. Yet the only drawback is the father also lives in America, and Sabrina is the apple of his eye. Gitte, that could be easily taken care of also. We could make an arrangement. He would always fly for free to Pharderma his whole life."

"Elsa, I can offer Brigitte her own suite with a complete kitchen and everything."

"Gitte, in this castle, only you have a suite like that. All the other suites have no kitchen."

"Well, I do want her to have all the comforts of having her own place. Well, it is time to call the architects if we want this done ASAP!"

"Elsa, I am so excited. Can you help me plan a Christmas Eve party? I would like to welcome them that way, with all the children of Pharderma enjoying Christmas together. I know they will criticize me.

I am throwing a party eleven days after my king/husband's burial, yet I don't care. It's my country. I do what I want."

Elsa replied, "Gitte, anything you want, I am here for you, yet it is getting late. I think I will sleep over tonight again, and I will sleep in Briana's room."

Gitte invited the pastor to join them for dinner; he accepted, feeling like all his pain was lifted. His soul was happy again; he even felt as if he could go back to being a doctor; he had been a great doctor. When Briana came home from dance practice and found that Auntie Elsa was there and they would have dinner together, Briana instantaneously brightened up, and then Auntie told her she was sleeping over too. Wow, she felt wonderful.

At dinner, Briana noticed that everyone was happy, not knowing why; it just made her feel good, and knowing Auntie Elsa was sleeping over again, plus her mommy was also all smiles. The last few days, her mommy was always crying, and Briana didn't know how to help her. Something was going on, yet Briana didn't care; it was something good.

Elsa had to talk to both girls. She knew that Sabrina came every night. Briana had told her that they played all kinds of games. Lately, they were playing what they called the Bond games (James Bond). When Sabrina showed up that night, she was also delighted to see Briana's aunt. She marveled at the resemblance to her own aunt, Auntie Elsie. Elsa asked Sabrina what she was doing for Christmas. Sabrina immediately brightened up and said she and her mom won a contest and they would be going to visit a tropical island for Christmas vacation and that she will miss her family, but getting away from the winter was a treat.

Elsa asked her, "What island will you be visiting?"

Sabrina cocked her head to one side and said, "Pharderma? I had never heard of that island before."

Elsa saw Briana start to brighten, and she shook her head. Briana understood immediately.

"Sabrina, it's getting late. You should be going."

Giving Elsa and Briana a hug and kiss, she stood up and said, "Home," and she was gone.

Briana turned to her auntie. "Auntie, why did we not tell Sabrina that this was Pharderma?"

"Because we want it to be a surprise, OK? They should be here in two days, on Christmas Eve, and guess what? We are planning a huge Christmas Eve party for all of Pharderma."

Briana was visibly confused. "But, Auntie, my daddy just died. How can we have a party?"

"Well, that's what your mommy wants, OK?"

"OK, I can't help but be excited. Auntie, I have to tell you something. I don't feel sad that my father died. Auntie, I didn't cry. I don't seem to feel anything."

Elsa told Briana, "Sometimes our bodies are in shock and it takes a long time to feel something. I think that's what happening to you."

"OK, Auntie. I was beginning to feel as if I wasn't normal."

"You are fine, sweetheart."

Elsa realized at that moment that she could not bear to have Briana live anywhere else but in Pharderma. *Wow, hopefully Brigitte would be willing to live here. If Briana were to leave, part of Elsa would go too.* Sighing, she took Briana in a deep hug. She prayed to God that Brigitte would realize that it was the king's fault this happened and that Briana was so much a part of their lives in Pharderma. When they pulled away, Elsa was crying. Briana thought she was crying for the king.

CHAPTER TWENTY-ONE

The castle was in a frenzy. Everyone was preparing for the upcoming Christmas Eve party. Cooks were preparing the delicious foods for the party. Entertainers were practicing their arts. The people of Pharderma didn't understand; not long ago, their king died, and now the queen's having a huge Christmas party? Shouldn't she be mourning? They even noticed that when she made a special television announcement about the party and that all the children of Pharderma are invited, she was wearing bright colors; their custom was to wear black or gray and white for one year. The people decided among themselves that the queen might have gone a little mad. Yet the children of Pharderma were all excited; they were told that each child would receive a gift. Indeed, the queen had her staff contact all the parents and even the orphanage to find out what every child truly wanted for Christmas. It was Elsa's job to make certain that the gift and the child were a match.

Elsa had asked her husband to bring some loose amethyst stones home. She found two stones of similar size. (Elsa had taken Briana's crown home with her.) Elsa was making an exact replica for Sabrina, plus she had to replace the amethyst stone for Briana's crown. On the morning of Christmas Eve, the jeweler called that everything was ready: two identical crowns, beautiful just like the girls; the center stone looked very much like the original stones, but there was no fire inside of them.

Brigitte and Sabrina's flight was to arrive at 9:34 p.m. The castle was ready; it was completely lit with white Christmas lights. People could see the castle from all points of Pharderma. Mood was changed; everyone was happy. (They all did feel slightly guilty; they had just lost their king, and they reasoned that in some cultures, people celebrated death, and maybe that's what their queen was doing.) The children were so happy; never in the history of Pharderma had there been a Christmas party for everyone inside the castle.

Elsa went with the chauffeur to pick up Brigitte and Sabrina at the airport.

When they arrived, Brigitte was excited. She felt renewed. They had treated her and Sabrina like a queen on the plane. Boy, she could get used to this. Waiting for their luggage, Sabrina was reading a book that she was given on the plane called *Cyrena Princess of the Sea,* and she was still engrossed in it. Brigitte looked up and saw Prince Stranoff. He was getting ready to board a plane. He had seen her first, and he was telling himself if he hadn't just left the castle and just spoken to Queen Gitte and seen Briana in her finery, he would have thought that this woman and her child were the queen and princess. The similarities were amazing.

Well, Brigitte had definitely seen Prince Stranoff; he was not a man to be missed at about five eight, medium build, with broad shoulders and golden-brown skin with curly black hair. The prince had a square jaw with a broad straight nose, almond-shaped eyes; his eyes were light brown with specks of yellow and eyelashes women dream off. He reminded Brigitte of the men in the Marines, with their erect and demanding persona. Sabrina was so engrossed in her book she didn't even notice. Finally, Brigitte saw their bags. Grabbing them, she told Sabrina to take hers. As she turned and looked up, she noticed a man with a banner with her name on it, with a woman that could easily pass for her sister Elsie. She walked to them and said, "I am Brigitte St. Phard."

Elsa said, "Welcome to Pharderma. I am Elsa, your guide."

Brigitte called Sabrina over. As soon as Sabrina saw Elsa, you could see she was excited. Elsa shook her head slightly, and Sabrina understood immediately. Looking down at Sabrina's feet, she had the purple shoes on. Walking over, she took her mother's hand.

"Sabrina, this is Elsa, our guide. Doesn't she look just like your auntie Elsie?"

Sabrina replied, "Yes, Mommy."

The chauffeur took their bags, and Elsa said, "This way, please."

To Brigitte's astonishment, there was a white limousine outside, and that's where her bags were going.

So far, she was surprised. Never in her life had she ever won something of this magnitude before. Sabrina, on the other hand, was extremely quiet. Elsa was pointing out landmarks, and Brigitte could see from a distance a huge structure with lights. As they got closer and closer, the structure turned out to be a huge castle, just like in the fairy tales she still reads to Sabrina. It seemed that they were heading in that direction. Suddenly Brigitte just got quiet and just listened to Elsa point at this or that. Butterflies had started to take their place in her stomach. She wanted to keep her hopes down, yet as they got closer and closer to this beautiful castle, it seemed that this was their destination. Arriving at the castle's huge gate, the noticed the wrought iron gate was the shape of a butterfly. So magnificent was the gate. The driver pressed a button, and it opened up. As they drove the long, winding road leading up to the castle, Brigitte took in the palace's night beauty, still feeling breathless and full of anticipation.

The limousine stopped, and Elsa announced, "Welcome to Castle St. Jude. This is where you will be staying for the duration of your holiday."

Sabrina found her voice and said, "This is a castle."

"Yes, it is, my dear, and Queen Gitte is inside, waiting to greet you."

Brigitte hadn't realized that she was holding her breath and let out a deep sigh. *OK,* she thought. *This also seems real.* As they approached the huge entry door, the wood was also carved in the shape of a butterfly. Brigitte thought, *They love butterflies here.*

Then the door was opened by a uniformed butler. He opened his arms and said, "Welcome to Castle St. Jude and home of Queen Gitte of Pharderma."

The huge entry was amazing with two spiral staircases with a huge Christmas tree in the middle. Children were everywhere, laughing, and somewhere someone was singing. The floor was marble, a beautiful light-green marble. The paintings on the walls looked so real; they looked alive. The drop-down chandelier shone like real diamonds. The palace was straight out of one of Sabrina's fairy-tale books. Sabrina's eyes opened wide to take it all in. Brigitte couldn't speak.

Elsa said, "You arrived on time for our Christmas party."

A petite woman in a beautiful flowing blue gown was descending the stairs. Brigitte looked at her with surprise. They said everyone had a twin, and Brigitte had just laid her eyes on hers. They were the same height, color, eyes, and hair; only thing was Brigitte was a little chestier.

Elsa said, "Queen Gitte, may I introduce to you Brigitte and Sabrina St. Phard."

"Hello, Brigitte and Sabrina St. Phard. I am so happy you are here. Welcome to Pharderma and to my home, Castle St. Jude. Arthur, would you please show them to their suite? Miss St. Phard, everything is set for you to freshen up, and please come join us in the Christmas Eve celebration."

"Yes, thank you, Queen Gitte. Please call me Brigitte."

"OK, Brigitte. We have a wonderful evening planned. I don't want you to miss anything, so please go freshen up."

Brigitte and Sabrina were taken to a very decorative double door. The butler pressed a button, and it was an elevator. Inside he pressed the third-floor button. The doors opened up to a beautiful hallway. They walked to a beautifully decorated door with gold handles. With a golden key, the butler opened the door to a lovely living room and an adjoining dining room; there was a full kitchen, an office, and three bedrooms.

They thanked the butler, and he handed Brigitte the golden key and said, "Do enjoy yourselves."As soon as the door closed, Brigitte and Sabrina held each other hands and just started jumping. Brigitte told Sabrina, "Can you believe this! A castle, a real castle."

"Yes, Mommy."

They looked around. The living room had a beautiful fireplace; the dining room had huge glass doors that opened up to a huge patio. They could see the mountains. The place was breathtaking.

"Mommy, let's hurry up and wash up so we can join the party."

"OK, baby, but I didn't' really bring any fancy clothes."

Just then, there was a knock on the door; it was Elsa with two big boxes.

Brigitte said, "What is this?"

Elsa replied, "A gift from the queen—something to wear tonight."

Brigitte said, "How did the queen know my size?"

"In New York, when you board the plane, a picture is taken of every passenger. We were able to estimate you and your daughter's size from those photos."

Brigitte finally said, "Wow, OK."

She took her box, and Sabrina took hers. They opened the boxes at the same time. Brigitte had a black dress with what looked like real diamonds on the neckline; it was long and fitted with a side slit. There was also a shoe box—black strappy sandals, it seems, with diamonds on them.

Sabrina opened her box, and inside was a lavender gown with little butterflies all over it, and it was sparkly. It matched her purple shoes perfectly. Elsa gave Sabrina a wink. Sabrina was so happy.

Brigitte was like, "Oh my god, the dress matches the purple shoes perfectly."

Elsa looked at Sabrina's shoes and told Brigitte, "Her heel is almost finished. While she bathes and gets ready, we can have the heels fixed. We have everything in the castle and on the castle grounds— cleaners, shoe repair, hair salon, fully staffed gym, movie theaters, church, tennis court, basketball court, and a field-size track. There is more, but you have time later to explore."

Brigitte said, "Yes, that would be a great idea."

Elsa mentioned, "We will be having a midnight Mass, and all the children will be receiving gifts from Santa after Mass in the entry hall by the Christmas tree."

Sabrina took off her shoes and gave them to Elsa. Elsa sighed all night; she was trying to figure out how she was going to get the shoes from Sabrina. Elsa needed to switch the stones. She had to put the glass purple stones back in. It was time to reclaim her amethyst stones. Before she brought them to the repairman, she had already switched the stones. It took all of five minutes to repair the shoes; they looked brand new again.

As Elsa walked back to Brigitte and Sabrina's suite, she speculated on everything that had happened in the last eight months and how it would boil down to what Brigitte wanted to do. Elsa could use the stones to help Brigitte's decision, but she felt that would be going over the boundaries. God did give us freedom of choice. All she could do was pray. Losing Briana wasn't a sweet feeling; Briana was like her fourth child. Arriving at their door, she knocked; no answer. Using the castle skeleton key, she let herself in and placed the shoes on Sabrina's box. She took a look around the expansive suite and thought, *It is beautiful. They would be happy here.* She left, feeling a little worried; the future was unpredictable.

It was eleven thirty on Christmas Eve; it seemed that all the children of Pharderma were in the castle. The castle hall had a thirty-foot Christmas tree. Under the tree was a gift for every child in Pharderma. Everywhere Elsa looked, children were playing. There were Santas everywhere and Santa's helpers. The children's laughter was like music to Elsa's ears.

Midnight Mass was to start soon. Elsa had also changed into a striking white gown. Hanging from her neck was one of her favorite pieces made from a flower amethyst stone with diamonds around it; her husband had given her this lovely necklace when she had turned forty (it was the same piece Jartine had wanted), and she wore it with earrings that she had her jeweler make for her from the small stones her husband had given her eight long years ago; even these small stones had that living fire in them. She felt amazing; words couldn't describe the feeling that these pieces did for her.

She went to check on Brigitte and Sabrina and knocked, and Sabrina asked, "Who is it?"

"It's Elsa."

When she opened the door, the second real-life princess stood before her. With her hand to her mouth, she gushed, "Sabrina, you look like a real-life princess."

Brigitte walked in from the bedroom and said, "That's what I call her all the time. She's my little princess."

Brigitte looked radiant. The diamonds on her dress shone with their own light; she looked happy—truly happy.

"So, ladies, are we ready? Midnight Mass is about to start in ten minutes."

Brigitte and Sabrina in unison told Elsa, "You look amazing."

Elsa felt so happy inside and outside—she felt everything was going to be all right—and replied with a sincere thank-you.

The mother and daughter locked arms and said, "Yes, we are ready."

Down the elevator, and they were in the great hall.

Sabrina hadn't noticed the tree before and said, "Mommy, look at the tree, and check out all the presents."

Elsa said, "All the children of Pharderma are here tonight, and there is a gift for each child here. That also includes you, Sabrina."

The loudspeaker came on, and it said, "Children, please make your way to the chapel. Mass will begin in five minutes."

All the children stopped what they were doing, and Elsa and the Santa's helpers helped to usher the children to the church. The queen was already there. Briana was also there, but no one could see her because the queen had her sitting next to her nanny Danise, and her nanny was a very plump woman.

At the stroke of midnight, the pastor, Ricardo Lestin, came out first. "Ladies and gentlemen, Merry, merry Christmas. So how are we all today?"

All the children replied in unison, "Great, happy, excited."

"Well, we have a lot to be thankful for. We have to say thank you to Queen Gitte for having this great Christmas party."

In unison, the children said, "Thank you, Queen Gitte."

Gitte nodded and waved, and the children were just so happy.

Mass lasted exactly thirty minutes. All the while Mass was going on, Brigitte was trying to jog her memory about the pastor. She knew him from somewhere; she had seen him before, but her mind couldn't pinpoint it. At the end, when everyone was leaving, Elsa asked Brigitte to please wait a moment. Nanny Danise had left with Briana through the other door. Neither Brigitte nor Sabrina hadn't seen Briana yet. When the church was empty except for the queen, pastor, and Elsa, they had all moved to where the queen was sitting. Elsa spoke to Brigitte. "I want to welcome you again to Pharderma. We just wanted to speak to you and Sabrina. I also would like you to keep an open mind.

"I must tell you it is more than chance that you have come to be here. Eight months ago, I was in New York with my husband. We went to eat at a popular place in Manhattan called the Olive Garden. That is where I first saw Sabrina and you. You see, eight years ago, something happened in this castle. The queen had delivered a stillborn baby girl, and she had passed out in the delivery room right after giving birth. Our king, her husband, King Sigor, was in complete rage. He had made a phone call then grabbed me and told me to bury my sister's child. I was also told that whatever I saw, if I was to tell anyone anything, something would happen to my three children.

"About four hours later, a baby girl was brought here, and when the queen awoke, she asked for her child, and the king gave her this baby girl. I could not tell my sister anything. For months, I listened for news in Pharderma for someone that lost a child on March 22, 2000. I checked out our obituary for that day to see if a mother had died giving birth. Nothing—I never found anything—not until I was in New York that day and I saw your daughter, Sabrina, an exact replica of my niece. It clicked right then and there why I never found anything. My niece Briana had to be a twin because this little girl is her replica.

"So the next day, I hired a private investigator. He found everything, and I was right. My niece and your daughter were indeed twins. So now I have this information, what should I do with it? The more I thought about it, the more I noticed that my niece's eyes always seemed sad. She was a princess. Why was she sad? The reason is because twins can feel each other. That's why also I believe you, Brigitte, as a natural mother, deserved to know you were carrying twins all along, yet neither you nor your doctor knew it at the time. Now my dilemma was the king, a man that can take another person's child. What are his limitations? If I were to go against the king, what would he do to me? Surely, I realized my life or my children's lives were in danger. But a force beyond my control was pushing me on. I had to find a way. I didn't know how, but there had to be a way."

Queen Gitte spoke. "Brigitte, I just learned all of this on December 21. That day was the worst day of my life. Elsa called me, saying she needed to speak to me. 'Why?' I asked. She didn't say. About two hours later, Elsa arrived with Pastor Lestin. Then she proceeded to tell me my daughter is not the child I gave birth to. I thought my sister hated me. I just lost my husband. King Sigor died on December 7, just three weeks ago. I felt that Elsa was trying to destroy me because Briana was all I had left, and now she was telling me that she isn't even mine. That night, I died several times over, plus Elsa had brought over Pastor Lestin. I couldn't understand why she had brought him along. Then he proceeded to tell me why he was here and the role he played in the conspiracy."

Pastor then spoke to Brigitte. "I don't know if you remember me, but I was your doctor during your pregnancy. I never knew you were carrying twins. We never saw two fetuses in your sonograms, nor did we hear two heartbeats. It wasn't until the nurse taking care of you suddenly heard a second heartbeat that I realized you were carrying twins. Maybe Briana was always behind Sabrina. I don't know why we didn't know.

"As soon as I had confirmed it for myself, I got a phone call. It was King Sigor demanding I find a baby and have one for him right away, or he would destroy everything I have built for myself in America, and he mentioned, 'Remember, it was my money that allowed you to start this thriving business.' So, you see, my dilemma. Here I have twins, and the mother or I never knew she was carrying them. It was perfect. No one would ever know the truth. So I told the nurse to clean up the first baby while I took care of the second baby, cleaning her up and footprinting her myself.

"As soon as I was done wrapping her up, there was a knock on the door...two men and a woman, demanding to give them the child. I handed her over with her papers. As I turned around, the nurse was staring at me agape, and she said, 'What have you done? Why did you give those people the other baby?'"I took the nurse aside and told her what she had just seen she has to forget it, or I would destroy her. Terrified, the nurse shook her head yes, she would forget this ever happened. After that, I went to tend to you, cleaning and stitching you up. Miss St. Phard, for eight years, I have been carrying this guilt inside of me. Up to five years ago, I couldn't practice medicine any longer, and I was an alcoholic and was abusing drugs, always trying to get rid of this guilt I carried every day. I took someone's child. I didn't deserve to be rich, to be respected as a doctor, so I gave it up, returned to Pharderma, and became a bum.

"The pastor of our church took me in. He cleaned me up and told me God had other plans for me, so I felt that God was giving me a second chance. I studied to be a pastor. Maybe, just maybe, God would erase my guilt. So when Elsa walked into my office that day on December 1 and said she had to speak to me, I felt it... she knew who I really was. She told me she had found you and you would be coming to Pharderma around Christmastime and I had to tell you the truth. I was terrified because I just knew the king would kill me, but when I heard the king had died, all I could think of was how was I going to tell my queen that her only child was not hers? Her husband had just died, and I was the one to break her heart. I just didn't think I could do it."

All the time, Brigitte never said a word; her mind was screaming, *Twins! I was carrying twins! No wonder I was so big. No wonder my face changed so much and I even had toxemia!*

Elsa walked to the door and opened it. Briana had been waiting with her nanny. Briana knew in her heart all along that Sabrina was her twin; she felt it, and why would Sabrina be coming to her every night? They were so much alike, and the connection was so strong. Briana ran to Sabrina, and they hugged—hugged for all their missed years. They both started to cry. In fact, everyone in the room was crying. Elsa knew only one thing—those two could never be apart again. It was all up to Brigitte now. Only she could decide what would happen to Briana. Elsa had the stones; they were in her pocket (her evening gown had pockets), and she could use them. Suddenly a loud speaker went on in Elsa's head: "Free will. I gave them free will!" *Oh, my God, OK, I understand. Free will, OK! I won't use the stones.*

Queen Gitte was dying and happy at the same time—happy because she always saw that sadness in Briana's eyes and now she knew why, and she also knew the sadness would be gone, happy also that Sabrina was also complete. Gitte was also dying that the child she loved from core of her being was not hers.

Brigitte had the power to take her away, and she would have every right to do that.

Brigitte got up then and went to her daughters, got on her knees, and touched Briana and Sabrina. They both had let each other go to hug their mom. They all were crying. She had two—all along, she had two. Elsa walked to the window and just looked up at the sky. The tears wouldn't stop; they came from deep within her core. The queen walked over to Elsa, and they held each other.

Brigitte let go of her girls and walked over to Elsa and the queen. "Queen Gitte, can we speak in private?"

Gitte said, "Of course."

They went into an adjacent room. Gitte decided to sit down; her legs had no more power. She didn't know what Brigitte would say.

"Queen Gitte—"

"Please just call me Gitte."

"Gitte, ever since my baby was born, I have always thanked God for her because that's the only good thing that came out of my marriage with her father. In order for her to be here, he had to be in my life. But for the last two years, since my marriage dissolved, I have been struggling with Sabrina in the States. After September 11, 2001, my life has changed drastically. Jobs are so hard to come by. From the beginning,

I've called Sabrina Princess—she has always been my little princess. I didn't know Briana even existed, yet she has been living the life of a real-life princess all along. The mother that she knows is a queen. The father that she knew was a king. New York is not really a place to raise a child, let alone two.

"I can't take a real princess and make her live a regular life. What I can do is let her continue to be the princess that she is and let her sister be a princess right along with her. Would that be OK with you? Gitte, can we stay, all three of us?"

Gitte just shook her head yes and broke down, crying, hugging Brigitte. "Thank you. Thank you so much. You will be happy here, and, yes, Sabrina was always a princess. We will raise them together.

Let's go tell them because I think my sister is about to have a heart attack from not knowing."

Both women came out of the room arm in arm. Everyone was on pins and needles. Elsa's nerves were taking on a life of their own. Gitte locked eyes with Elsa and smiled. Brigitte went to the girls and asked Sabrina, "You want to stay here?"

Sabrina, with tears flowing down her face, said, "Yes, Mommy."

Elsa said, "Well, ladies and gentlemen, I guess it's time to join the party."

The two girls locked arms and walked out the door together.

Under the Christmas tree, Elsa pulled out two gifts; she gave one to each girl. They opened it. Briana got her crown back with the large middle stone back in place, and Sabrina got an identical crown. Elsa said to Sabrina, "You were always a princess, you just didn't know it yet." She took each girl's crown and set them upon their heads while Queen Gitte and Brigitte watched.

Standing alone, watching the two princesses playing with each other and Queen Gitte speaking to Brigitte, both women laughing, Elsa just smiled to herself; the real purple stones were in her pocket.

Her secret—no one could ever know about the power of the stones and the part that the purple shoes played.

THE END.